Confessions of a Bleeding Heart

Part 1

A once broken and lost girl.

Her desperate search for love and happiness.

Can a lost soul find her way back toward the light?

ISBN: 9798332999130 (Paperback)

Front book cover design by Quardeay Julien.

Back book cover design by Iesha Bree.

Editing and formatting by MasterPieces Writing and Editing LLC.

Printed in the United States of America.

First printing edition 2024.

keontapolk@outlook.com

To my kids and everyone who helped me become the woman I am today . . .

Acknowledgments

I want to thank my parents, Gloria Baskerville and Brandyn Cagle, for always being there for me. For never making me walk through life alone. For never giving up on me and always showing me unconditional love.

To Shanti Gordon, Lopez Robinson, Toya Gordon, Marcia Warren, and Courtney Woodard, thank you for always being there for me. For staying on me, pushing me, encouraging me, supporting me, and motivating me to finish this book and get it out to the world.

And to my editor and book coach, Erica James, thank you for being by my side the whole way and for never giving up on me. You also constantly pushed me, motivated me, and encouraged me. It's been a long journey, but you stayed down with me through it all, and for that, I'm so thankful God allowed our paths to cross.

Contents

Prologue i
Chapter 1 1
Chapter 2 9
Chapter 3 16
Chapter 4 26
Chapter 5 36
Chapter 6 47
Chapter 7 61
Chapter 8 80
Chapter 9 91
Chapter 10 101
Chapter 11 113
Chapter 12 127
Chapter 13 138
Chapter 14 164
Chapter 15 176
Chapter 16 193
About the Author 211

Disclaimer:

Though inspired by true events, the characters in this book are a product of the author's imagination. Names and identifying details have been changed to protect the privacy of any individuals involved. This book also contains instances of sexual abuse and domestic violence, which may be triggering for some readers.

Prologue

It is early in the morning, and I am sitting all alone on the porch, listening to the birds chirping. I can smell the early morning dew, and I can hear the constant voices in my head, telling me I am a blessed little girl with such a wonderful life. I have a mother who loves me more than anything in the world and a father who would do nothing less than die for me. He caters to me with his love and with plenty of his time, something all little girls need from their fathers.

As a smile covers my face, I continue getting lost in thought, trying to convince myself that I am so happy inside and there is no one who I would rather be than me. I have the same things most little girls have. I have new clothes, new shoes, all the newest baby dolls, and even a pink bedroom decorated just right.

The sun beams on my face as I giggle inside. I see myself having fancy birthday parties with cute Barbie decorations, presents, snacks, and all my friends having the most fun little girls can imagine having. I even think about how someone could not love the life I am living. Yes, I have it all, until I take a look around and realize this is not my reality.

These thoughts are only my hopes and dreams from deep within. They haunt me, making me believe I can have them, but in my case, I am a broken little girl whose hopes and dreams seem out of reach. A little girl who has endured so much pain at such a young age. The agony of the pain haunts my soul. Tears fill my eyes as I think about the terror that cripples my body. Misery, anger, and disgust rush through my body as I sit here, wishing my life could be a normal one. Though I often drift to another place filled with peace and happiness, I always have to come back to earth and accept the reality of my world.

-Keren ♥

Chapter 1

Momma sure does work a lot, I thought to myself as I watched my mother, Gina, get my little brother Darnell ready to visit my grandmother. In 1988, it was just me and my brother back then, as far as my mother's kids. I am two years older than Darnell, and I cannot deny it seemed as if my brother was always my mother's favorite child. He was her baby. She showed him so much attention and love. My brother was a momma's boy, for sure. If she was lying down or sitting on the couch, my brother would be right up under her, acting spoiled, while I would sit there in envy, giving him the evil eye.

It usually took a while for us to get dressed during those days because my brother and I were young kids and my mother needed to cook and clean the house before getting the three of us together. I often sat and watched her, thinking about all the exhausting things she must do daily as a grown-up, and I was thankful I was still a child. After witnessing what my mother went through, I doubted if I ever wanted to be an adult.

My mother was a beautiful black woman with a golden complexion. Most black people would refer to her as a redbone. She was about 5'5" with long black hair and a body that many women would kill for. Everyone thought my mother was so gorgeous, and that I looked just like her. I agree; I am a spitting image of my mother. She is just lighter than me.

I often wondered how a woman so beautiful could settle for a man who barely loved her. You would think he had to love her because he married her, but his actions were not those of love. There was nothing but a heartless soul that lived inside of Bernard, my stepfather. Though I saw him as a man once upon a time, he was nothing but the devil in my eyes.

"Mom, what's wrong," I asked her as I watched her hide the bruise that marked her beautiful face.

"I'm okay," she told me.

I knew it was a lie because that was not the first time I had seen bruises on my mother's face. Hiding the marks Bernard left on her face and body had become a part of her daily routine. She also pretended as if she was the only woman in his life. That was a lie, too.

"You kids get your stuff together so I can walk you down to your grandma's house," Mom panted as she spoke to me and my brother, her demeanor a little different this time.

As we gathered our things, I observed my mom as she walked into her room and adjusted the temperature on her waterbed. She turned the knob to the highest setting and then tiptoed over to the window and locked them before tiptoeing out of the room, pad-locking the door behind her. I watched her in amazement because the look on her face communicated she either wanted to kill Bernard or burn him up.

"Mom, what are you doing?" I asked, confused.

"Girl, didn't I tell you to get your things together? Now hurry your ass up," she urged, still rushing through the house.

I stopped asking questions, but I continued observing her because I had already gathered my things. Now, my mother was turning the heat all the way up on the thermostat in the house. She walked through our home, making sure all the windows were locked, and then she hurried us out the door.

As we walked down the street to my grandma's house, my little mind wondered what was going to happen to Bernard, not out of care for him, but out of concern for my mother.

The look on my mother's face appeared to be a mixture of anger, disappointment, sadness, and exhaustion. Until that moment, the only other time I had noticed sadness in her eyes was about two years prior, when my grandfather's lover had killed him on Christmas day.

I will never forget that moment. I was almost four years old, and once again, we went to grandma's house for Christmas. When we walked in, I could feel the hurt that filled my grandma's apartment. My uncles and my grandmother were crying hysterically.

"Dad is dead!" one of my uncles cried as we walked through the door.

I never met my grandfather, so I was not hurt by his passing. However, I was sad because my family, especially my mother, was in so much pain. Even though I did not understand the severity of the situation, I knew that memory would stick with me for the rest of my life. I also knew Christmas would never be the same. Little did I know, my life would never be the same because of another life-changing event, something much worse.

♥

Just about every day, we followed the same routine. We would get up, eat breakfast, and get ready to go over to my grandma's house for the day, but our mornings usually involved some type of argument between Bernard and my mom. Some days differed from others, especially when we would have a nice and quiet morning, but those days were few and far between.

"I'm heading to work," my mother said one morning.

"Are we going over to grandma's house today?" I asked.

"No, Ernest will be coming here to watch you and your brother till I get off."

My mom looked at me, noticing the fear and disappointment wash over my face.

"It won't be that bad," she reassured me.

With my heart pounding and hands sweating, I sat there, thinking, *Yeah, your brother says the same thing*.

I was five years old and carrying the biggest secret of my life. Instead of playing hopscotch or tag like the other little girls, I was being forced to engage in inappropriate acts with my mom's brother, Ernest. Ernest was one of my mother's younger brothers. He was the second youngest, but never my favorite. Because my family was close, he was always around us, and everyone loved him just like any other family member, but that was also because they did not know he was a pedophile and a rapist.

Before the molestation, Ernest appeared to be a stand-up type of guy. He would walk me to and from school to ensure I made it home safely, which always made me feel loved and secure. That feeling did not last long.

With just one deplorable act, feelings of confusion, hurt, terror, endangerment, and hate had replaced it.

It all started with little touches, like tickling me on my sides and stomach. I know it may sound harmless, but the tickles were not as innocent as they seemed. "Stop," I would say as I laughed and squirmed, trying to get away from him, but then I would feel his hands move down to my private areas. He would laugh like he was still playing, but it was not funny to me because I knew he was not supposed to be touching me there. I was young, so I did not understand how I was supposed to feel about the situation. The person violating me was supposed to be someone who protected and loved me, not someone who harmed me.

I can remember lying there, smelling the stale smell of alcohol on his breath as he kissed me on my lips. Tears streamed down my face as I looked up at him and wondered why. Why would he do this to me?

"Please stop," I pleaded through my cries.

"You love me, don't you," he replied, his funky mouth hovering over my body. "It's not going to be that bad, and this is our little secret. If you tell anyone, we both will get in trouble, and you don't want that do you?" he continued as I lay there frozen with fear, tears still streaming down my face.

Ernest moved from kissing my lips to kissing my private parts. Then the kissing progressed to him taking his fingers and playing with areas that were off-limits to everyone. Even though I was young, I remember my teacher informing us about good touches and bad touches at school one day. It did not take much to realize my uncle's touches were bad touches. Any time we were alone, Ernest would use that time to turn my little body into his nasty playground.

"Time to play our game," he said once. "Lay down."

I complied because I did not want to make Ernest mad, nor did I want to get into any trouble. He said he would make things worse for me, and I believed him. I lay there on the couch with tears welling in my eyes, looking up at my uncle, hoping he would change his mind or that someone would walk through the door and catch him. Then he would go away to jail, and I would not have to deal with the torture anymore.

He climbed over me and started pulling my pants and panties down. I lay there so stiff that you would have thought I was paralyzed, but that is exactly how I felt, like a little girl able to walk but just too afraid to make any moves. Soon after, I could feel my uncle's rough, scratchy hands rubbing all over my body. I felt his fingers go in between my legs and rub on my cookie jar. I instantly tensed up, and the tears rolled down my face like a waterfall.

"Do you like that?" he asked.

I shook my head no, but that did not make him stop what he was doing. It seemed like my response challenged him to do more. Even after I shook my head no to his question about liking how he violated me, he began licking and kissing my cookie jar. Again, I asked Ernest to please stop, but he ignored my cries and continued to do more.

Lying there, feeling disgusted, humiliated, and like a piece of trash, I felt Ernest take his fingers and spread my cookie jar apart and what seemed to be something enormously big trying to force itself inside of me. It was the most excruciating pain that my little body ever felt. I burst out screaming and crying because I was in so much pain; the man who was supposed to love and protect me was ripping my body apart. He took his hand and covered my mouth while he told me to be quiet.

"You want to get in trouble? You better be quiet and be quiet now," he said as he tried to force himself inside of me again.

All I could think about was how badly I wished someone would kill this monster of a man I was supposed to call my uncle.

♥

I often wondered if my family knew about Ernest and just never said anything. I could not understand how they did not know. Could they not see my face when I was around him, or how quiet and detached I became when he came around? When I used to travel places and see another little girl, I would think, *Is this little girl also dealing with a monster uncle? Has she, too, been touched and raped by someone who was supposed to love and protect her?* I even wondered if that little girl could look at me and tell I had endured the same thing, too.

Even though I was only a little girl, I felt so worthless. I felt like I was living with this pain alone, and no one understood how I felt or even cared about the pain and anger bottled up inside of me. I often wondered, *Why me?*

Before one of my favorite aunts passed away, I remember sitting down with her once. Aunt Shirley was a gorgeous woman whose presence would make everyone in a room turn around and stare at her in awe. Almost intuitively, she asked me if I had ever dealt with someone molesting me. At first, I was terrified to say anything because I could hear my uncle's voice in my head saying we would both get in trouble. Finally, I broke into tears and told her, "Yes."

"Who touched you?" she asked.

I looked her dead in the eyes and laid my head in her arms. "Uncle Ernest."

Her eyes widened. "Have you told anyone else?"

"No, I'm scared," I admitted.

My auntie was the most loving, compassionate, and understanding woman I had ever met in my life. She held me while I cried, kissed my forehead, and told me that what had happened was not my fault. I was just a little girl, and my uncle knew better. She told me I should not be afraid because he was very wrong for what he did and that I needed to talk to my mom and tell her. Though it made sense, talking to my mom was easier said than done. My mother was not an easy person to talk to . . . at all. I honestly thought she would not believe me, make it my fault somehow, or just push it under the rug, so I kept my mouth shut for years. I kept my mouth shut for most of my life.

Chapter 2

Though my childhood was unlike the average kid's, it had its moments. During most summers, I traveled to Indiana to visit my uncle Chip and my aunt Shirley, and I must say, being with my aunt and uncle was the best time of my life. In Indiana, I could be a little girl with no worries. I could play with my cousins all summer, and I did not have to worry about being violated, at least for a couple of months.

My aunt and uncle were the most important people in my life, and I looked forward to the summer all year long. Uncle Chip would take us kids out to the country and let us drive the country roads, which is how I learned to drive. He would also take us camping, fishing, and swimming.

Uncle Chip not only exposed us to nature, but he also instilled in us a good work ethic. One summer, he took me and my cousins to the local middle school and dropped us off with a loaf of bread, a family size bag of chips, a pack of bologna, and a gallon of juice so that we could work detasseling corn. Though we lasted only one day, it was a great work experience for a child, one I will always remember.

While there in Indiana, I could live freely as a child until my mother made me come back home at the end of the summer. Every year, I would pray and wish that year would be the year she allowed me to stay in Indiana with my aunt and uncle and attend school there. But every year, the answer was no. And shortly after, I would be back in Illinois, back with my abuser.

♥

The rape continued into the 90s until I was about ten years old. The only time I felt any relief was when my older stepsister, Tamara, Bernard's daughter, was around. When she was around, the molestation shifted from me to her. As bad as the thought was, I used to be so happy when it was her turn because I was no longer on my uncle's radar. I did not know for a fact that he was molesting her, but I noticed he would look at her with lust in his eyes. He would have her sit on his lap all the time, and he used to send us to the front room to watch TV while he made her come to the bedroom with him. They used to be in the bedroom for a long time, and when she returned, she always wore the same sad look on her face that I used to have when the violation was over. I hated that she was enduring the agony and pain I had experienced, but I was also relieved that it was her turn and not mine. I was happy that my little body could rest and that the predator's eyes were set on my older, yet still young, sister instead of me.

"That is so disgusting," Tamara said randomly one day.

"What are you talking about?" I asked. We were watching a movie, but I did not understand what she was referring to.

While pointing at the TV, Tamara explained, "That man right there was raping his stepdaughter while the mother was at work."

A combination of sadness and anger spread across Tamara's face. Though she did not utter a word, I knew why she looked that way. The look covered my face, too.

"Yeah, that is very disgusting, and I hope he goes to jail," I said.

My stepsister turned and looked at me, and we shared twin expressions of sadness. After a minute or two, we returned our gaze to the TV screen and continued watching the movie.

♥

My uncle's actions not only terrified me but also caused me to grow up with so much pain, resentment, and hatred in my heart. I blamed everyone around me for what my uncle did to me, and I used to wish him dead whenever I saw him. I now know I have to forgive him to heal completely, but I was not trying to hear that back then.

As fate would have it, Ernest spent plenty of time in and out of prison for other crimes and suffered from a severe case of diabetes. I did not feel sorry for him at all. How could I?

"Your uncle Ernest is not feeling well today. He is very sick," my mother told me one day.

Instantly, I shrugged my shoulders and gave her the "who-pooted face" because I could not care less about his well-being. *Why in hell would I care about how he is feeling when he is the reason I'm feeling all messed up inside?*

I guess my mother did not have her maternal instinct turned on because instead of her perceiving my body language as something being wrong, she must have perceived it as me being disrespectful.

"You shouldn't be like that," she responded. "God don't like ugly."

I thought to myself, *Well, he definitely doesn't like your brother or your husband then.*

While I love my mother with all my heart and soul, I would not be telling the truth if I said I never thought we could be closer, being that we are only fifteen years apart. Growing up, my relationship with my mother was not what I saw in other mother-daughter relationships. I would see other little girls having mommy-and-daughter dates. I would notice how happy other little girls seemed when they were with their mothers, laughing and playing games, hugging and telling each other "I love you". Those observations made it painfully obvious that my mother and I did not have that kind of relationship.

My resentment toward my mother grew stronger over the years because I could never understand how a mother could let someone sexually abuse her daughter. I felt as if she should have known what was going on, and she should have protected me from her demon brother.

Besides dealing with sexual abuse at the hands of her brother, I also had to deal with mental abuse from watching Bernard physically abuse and cheat on her. He also verbally abused us kids. Though my mother did not always say it, I know it affected her deeply.

"Y'all get up and throw some shoes on," my mother yelled as she cut on the bedroom light one night.

"Where are we going?" I asked, rubbing the sleep from my eyes.

"None of your business. Just do as I said," she ordered.

It was late at night, and my brother, my stepsister, and I were in bed asleep, until my mother woke us up. We did not know where we were going, but we did as my mother told us to do. We put on our shoes and our coats and met my mother at the front door, still wearing our cartoon pajamas. Moments later, we all climbed into Bernard's new truck and headed out of the driveway.

Still groggy, I kept my eyes open enough to pay attention to where we were going. Confusion spread across my face when we pulled up to some apartments I did not recognize. Later, I found out the apartment belonged to the "other woman".

We pulled into the parking lot of the apartment building, and my mother inched the truck up to the door, facing the woman's apartment with the bright lights on.

I asked my mother who lived there, but, of course, she ignored me. She put the truck in park and began smashing her foot against the gas pedal, ramming the gas. My mother would stop for a split second and then continue ramming the gas and holding her hand on the horn. Though it seemed like forever, my mother's shenanigans lasted about ten minutes before Bernard flew out of the apartment, upset that my mother had shown up in his new truck, trying to blow the motor out of it.

Looking like he had just thrown on some clothes, Bernard ran out there, cussing and going off on my mom. I was so upset because I could hear the argument and knew he was out cheating on my mother. She had just caught him damn near in the act. I wanted to protect her so badly, but what could I do, being a little girl and all?

More than anything, I remember seeing the hurt and pain in my mom's eyes as she defended herself from Bernard. I just wanted to jump out of the truck, attack Bernard, and hug my mother. Even though I felt sorry for my mom, I could not understand why she would allow this man to treat her like garbage when she was worth so much more and plenty of men would have loved to love her properly. I could not understand how she could love a man whose soul was so cold and whose demons were so evil. Though I empathized with her, I resented her for settling for this devil. Yet, I figured his day would come. Karma would catch up with him, and he would pay for what he had done and the pain he had caused . . . just like someone else I knew.

I hated thoughts of Ernest followed me everywhere I went, even when I tried not to think about him or the disgusting things he did to me. I questioned everyone and everything, especially adults.

♥

One thing I could count on was my relationship with my brother. We were always together. It was just me and him at the time, so he was my best friend. No matter how mad we were, we would never tell on each other when we did something wrong. My brother was my everything.

He once had this Bill Cosby doll that he loved and I hated. One day, while playing on my aunt's porch in the projects, I dangled the doll in front of him, teasing him. He yelled at me, demanding me to give it back to him, but I refused because he carried that ugly doll everywhere.

"That's why Uncle Ernest don't like you," my brother snapped.

His words immediately lit a fire in me. I thought, *If he doesn't like me, why won't he just leave me alone? Why does he keep touching me? Or maybe that's why he does it? Because he doesn't like me?*

My mind wandered as I became more upset, thinking about what my brother had said and how he received better treatment than I did. Unsure of what to do with my increasing anger, I took my frustrations out on my brother. I pushed him off the porch, and he fell, splitting his head open.

Mom ran out of the house after hearing my brother scream. "What did you do?" she asked frantically.

"He started it and pushed me, so I pushed him back," I lied. I was mad at my brother and wanted to hurt him simply because he had hurt me. And the worst part? He had to be rushed to the hospital to get stitches.

As I watched my brother crying hysterically, I instantly became sad because I knew my brother did not say those words to hurt me. I knew my brother truly loved me. At that moment, I felt so horrible and vowed never to hurt anyone who genuinely loved me. I only wished my family felt the same.

Chapter 3

"You kids sit down. I need to talk to you two," my mother told me and Darnell, six months after the Bernard incident.

"What's going on? What's wrong, mom?" I asked.

She hesitated and then spoke, "I want to tell you that I am leaving Bernard, and we are moving to Indiana."

Instantly, my face filled with excitement. My mother's announcement was the best news ever. Being near Uncle Chip and Aunt Shirley was the only time I could feel like a child. I was so happy about the move that I was ready to leave the next day. I was finally getting away from my monster of an uncle for good . . . or so I thought.

Within a matter of weeks, we moved into our house in Indiana, and it was great, except my mom was never home. Luckily, we lived around the corner from my aunt and uncle, whose house I visited often. To get there, I would walk through the alley where a man named Sabrina lived. Yes, a man named Sabrina. He would dress up in a halter top shirt and skirt looking just like a woman, and he would wear stars all over his body that he drew in with a marker.

While Uncle Skeeter was babysitting my brother and me one day, I asked him if I could ride my bike over to Uncle Chip and Aunt Shirley's house to see my cousins. Uncle Skeeter was my favorite uncle out of my mom's brothers. He loved me so much and would do anything in the world for me. He was my heart, and I was his.

"Yes, but be careful and go straight over there and be back before it gets dark," he warned.

I nodded and darted out of the house to jump on my bike.

While riding to my aunt and uncle's house, I cut through the alley like I always did, and out jumped Sabrina from his hiding place behind a garbage can. I stopped in my tracks, just staring at him. As he strode toward me, I got so scared that I jumped off my bike and took off running toward our house. I dashed into the house, terrified and out of breath.

"What's wrong with you," Uncle Skeeter asked, his eyebrows knitting together.

"Sabrina just tried to get me, and I left my bike in the alley," I told him.

My uncle's jaw tightened as veins popped out on his neck. Clearly, he was pissed.

"What do you mean, he tried to get you?"

I told my uncle what happened, and he flew out of the house, furious. While I do not know what was said or what happened, I know my uncle came back with my bike.

Unfortunately, I did not see my cousins that day. I was too traumatized to venture out again.

♥

Not only did Uncle Skeeter love me, but he also loved the mess out of his sister Gina, my mom. The whole family loved my mom deeply, but I wondered why that love resulted in so many people getting hurt on the day a guy at the park made a big mistake. In what seemed like an instant, the summer barbeque at our house took a turn for the worse.

"Where did Gina go?" my mom's boyfriend asked my cousin.

"She ran to the store with Tina," my cousin responded.

My cousin chuckled and then leaned over to my other cousin and whispered, "I think that's where she went."

"You know Gina didn't go to no dang on store. Her butt probably riding through the park," my other cousin said.

At that moment, my cousin Tina and my mom walked through the door, and it seemed as if Tina were out of breath. All I could hear was my mom trying to keep Tina from saying what she wanted to say. Panting, Tina finally let the words slip out of her mouth.

Tina told the men of my family and my mom's boyfriend that a man had knocked a drink out of my mom's hand at the park. Immediately, the energy in the house shifted. The men became angry, and they were ready to unleash their anger on the guy at the park and his crew. Everyone left the house and rushed over to the park where they spotted their target, some dudes from another city.

The scene at the park seemed like something out of a movie. There was so much fighting. People fighting with bats and bottles. People fighting with their fists. I could not believe the bloodbath that had taken place just because of a drink. People even had plugs of skin bitten out of their skin. The entire scene made me sick to my stomach. I was so terrified. I was even afraid of my family because I was certain we were part of a horror film. That horrific event was one I would never forget, and one that would haunt my life for a long time.

Months had passed since the fight when I walked into the living room to find my mom packing up our belongings in a big brown box.

"Mom, what are you doing? Why are you packing up our things?"

As I watched my mom in confusion, she spoke the words I feared the most, "We are moving back to Illinois."

When the words escaped my mom's lips, it felt like my heart had stopped and I struggled to breathe. I could not believe I was about to go from living my life as a child to having to face the monster again. I cried uncontrollably and pleaded with my mom to let me stay in Indiana.

"Mom, I don't want to go back to Indiana," I begged. "Can I please stay in Indiana with Uncle Chip?"

"No, you will be going back with me," she barked. The finality of her words sent a dagger through my heart.

I did not want to tell my mom why I wanted to stay in Indiana. I felt as if she should have known why I did not want to go back home.

After living in Indiana for two years, my mom, my brother, and I moved back to Illinois, the "Ill State". I called it the Ill State because so many horrific memories happened there. Fearing the worst, I could not help but think the molestation would continue as soon as we touched back down.

♥

Though not ecstatic about the move back home, I found a little comfort in going over to my uncle Jimmy's house. Jimmy was another one of my mother's brothers.

He was married to a woman who had a daughter my age, so I practically lived at their house. I enjoyed being at Uncle Jimmy's house because I did not have to deal with his other brother, the nasty rapist. I wanted to live with my uncle because he looked out for me. He took care of me until the day one of his stepsons made me feel like I was an intruder.

My step aunt Lisa and Uncle Jimmy dropped us off at Lisa's mom's house for a sleepover one night. When I got out of the car, Uncle Jimmy's stepson, Sam, said, "Why you always at our house, and why do you have to follow us everywhere we go?"

I just looked at Sam and wondered why he was talking to me in that way.

Even at a young age, I knew when I was unwanted. I told him, "I wasn't even staying. I'm going home."

I lied to Sam because I actually wanted to stay, but not after feeling like I was a burden. I was so hurt because no one understood what I was going through, nor why I did not want to be at home. It seemed like I had nowhere else to go.

With my heart feeling heavy, I walked back to the car and told Uncle Jimmy I was going home, and that was the last time I stayed over at my uncle's house.

♥

Even though I was completely unaware of it at the time, being back in the Ill State came with a big surprise. At nine years old, I learned about the man who was supposedly my biological father. I remembered meeting him only once or twice before. I could not remember what he looked like, but I remembered the car he drove. It was a dark blue, mid-size car, and its license plate spelled O WEST.

My mom, Darnell, and I lived on the south end of town when I crossed paths with my biological father. I was out in the neighborhood selling candy bars for school one day when I stumbled upon a house with my dad's car parked in the driveway. When I knocked on the door, a woman came to the door.

"Can I help you?" she said.

"Yes, I am with Glen Oak school, and I wanted to know if you would like to buy some candy bars to help our school out," I replied.

"How much are you selling them for?" the woman asked.

"One dollar, please."

She told me to give her a second, and she walked away from the door. I stood on the porch looking down at the car thinking, *Wow, that looks like the same car, and it has the same name on it*. As I waited, I wondered if this house could be where my dad lived, or if he was just visiting. I even wondered if I should say something or just leave and go home.

Snapping me out of my thoughts, the woman returned to the door and said, "I will take five of them."

My eyes lit up, and I said, "Thank you, ma'am."

After handing the woman her candy bars, I walked off the porch, kicking myself because I should have said something to her about the man whose car was parked at her house.

Even with so many thoughts running through my head, I walked around the corner smiling, as the reality of my discovery hit me. When I got home, I rushed through the door to tell my mom what had just happened.

"Girl, why are you running through here?" my mom asked, her tone reminding me to slow my pace.

"I was out selling candy, and I went to this house, and I think my dad lives there," I told my mom, nearly out of breath.

"Girl, what are you talking about?" she said, her face scrunched up.

"The house I went to around the corner had my dad's car in the driveway," I exclaimed.

My mom hesitated and then asked, "Did you see him?"

"No," I replied. "But can I go back out tomorrow and sell some more candy?"

She watched me carefully, as if questioning my motives.

Batting my eyes, I added, "Pleeeeeaaaaasssssseeee?"

After pleading with my mom for a few minutes, she agreed to let me go. I told my mom I was going to sell more candy, but I had other plans. I told myself I was going to go back to that house to see if that car was still there, and if so, I was going to knock on the door and ask for my dad.

When night fell, I could not sleep a bit. My stomach was in knots, and I was so anxious for the morning to come. It seemed like the night before Christmas, and I was ready to jump up and open my presents. *Why is the night taking forever?* is all I kept thinking about as I lay there in my bed.

The next morning finally arrived, and I was so excited. *Today is the day*, I thought. I jumped up out of the bed so quickly that you would have thought I was trying to hurry up and catch the school bus because I overslept. In record speed, I washed my face, brushed my teeth, combed my hair, and put on my cute blue jean shorts with a pretty pink t-shirt. I wanted to make sure I looked my best. After walking around the corner nervously, I approached the house, staring at the same car parked in the driveway.

Well, it's now or never, I thought. My heart pounded, and my stomach ached from the thought of walking up to the door looking for my dad and possibly being rejected.

Taking a deep breath, I knocked on the door, and the same woman came to the door again and asked, "How can I help you?"

I told the woman, "My name is Keren, and I was wondering if Oliver is here?"

The woman looked at me confused and said, "Yes, and can I tell him who is asking for him?"

"I am his daughter," I said.

Confusion spread across the lady's face again as she responded, "Hold on." She walked away from the door and returned a few seconds later. "Come in," she said.

I eagerly followed the woman into the house. When I stepped in, I thought to myself, *Wow, what a nice house she has.* Though somewhat small, it was bright and clean. The aroma of a lavender candle tickled my nose as I walked through the house. When the lady stopped walking, I looked up to see we were standing in front of the bathroom, where my dad was bending over to fix something. My dad turned around and looked at me with wide eyes, and then he gave me a warm hug. Seeing my dad coupled with him being excited to see me was the best feeling in the world. It felt like security, love, and wholeness all wrapped up into one.

Later, I learned the woman who had answered the door was my dad's wife. She made me feel at home. She would come to my house and pick me up on the weekends, and I would spend nights at their house. Her daughter and

I would have sleepovers, watch movies snuggled up with our snacks, and even wake up early on Sunday mornings and catch the church bus to Sunday service. It seemed like she was my real sister, and I loved going over to their house. My dad would go to my basketball games and take me on their family trips. We even went to Six Flags in St. Louis once. While I enjoyed the atmosphere with what seemed to be endless food and rides, I enjoyed being in my father's presence the most.

For the moment, I would be happy, but the sadness would creep in when our time together ended. I wished my dad could save me from the terror of my uncle. I figured if only I could stay with him when my mom left for work, then I could escape the torture. Even while enjoying my father's company, I silently prayed Uncle Skeeter would be at the house when I returned so that I could be protected and remain untouched.

♥

Uncle Skeeter being there for me was short-lived because he went to prison right before I turned eleven years old in 1994. He was on the run because he shot someone, and it finally caught up with him. Now he was being taken away from me. I was not there when the police took him away, but I knew it was coming.

One day, Uncle Skeeter came over and sat me down. He looked at me with sadness in his eyes and said, "I love you, and I will always love you, but Uncle has to leave you for a while."

I did not understand what he was telling me, but he continued, "I did something wrong, and I have to go away for a while." He paused. "I will be back home soon, and I will write to you every day."

Hurt and confused, I cried, wondering why this was happening to me. Why was my safety net leaving me in this world alone? You would have thought Uncle Skeeter was my dad as close as we were, and when he got locked up, it was the most hurtful thing for me. I know it was not his fault because he was protecting his sister, but I blamed him for leaving me alone. Through the pain and disappointment, I wrote to my uncle every single day, hoping each letter would keep us connected in spite of his absence.

I remember the prison having a family day, and my grandmother, Uncle Jimmy, and I went to visit Uncle Skeeter. There were so many inmates there, separated from their families. As I looked around, I saw men hugging their families, some smiling and others crying. I saw them engaging in games and eating food and playing with the kids. I sat there watching them, wondering what they could have done to be put in that cage, to be torn away from their families, and what was so important that they would sacrifice their freedom for it.

My uncle interrupted my thoughts when he snuck up behind me and said, “Hey, Niecy”. I turned around and leaped into my uncle’s arms.

It felt so refreshing to see him, hug him, and kiss him. We had so much fun being there with him for that short period of time, and it broke my little spirit when we had to leave him there. Being around my uncle made me forget about all my problems. Uncle Skeeter was like my superman, and he could do no wrong in my eyes. As I said goodbye to him, I cried so hard that my grandma had to grab my arm and pull me away from him. I sat in the backseat and cried myself to sleep the entire way home.

Chapter 4

"If you're done eating, empty your plates into the trash. Don't just leave your plates on the table," I told my brother as he headed out of the kitchen one evening.

Darnell turned around and inched back to the table to get his plate. Though he looked slightly disappointed, he emptied his scrapings into the trash and put his plate in the sink.

At eleven years old, I found myself having to be more of a big sister than a normal eleven-year-old should have to be. I had to babysit my little brother Darnell and now my little sister, Precious. Already feeling like I did not see my mom enough, I saw her even less during those days.

When my mom was not at home, she left us with my aunt and a couple of my uncles who lived with us occasionally, but they were not the best adults for children to be left alone with. They spent most of their time drinking and getting high. We did not have many things, but what little we did have would magically disappear, and we knew my relatives would steal it and then sell it to buy drugs. They would even steal the gifts my mom bought us for Christmas.

One morning, I woke up excited to watch the new TV my mom had bought me for Christmas, only to find it missing. Everyone said they did not know what happened to it, but I knew. Yes, I was young, but I was not stupid. My mom was already barely able to get us anything, and they stole the one present I did have. I sat there looking at my family crazily, repeating in my head, *I hope you pay for this.*

With our relatives living with us, I saw some things no child should ever see. Locked out of the house one chilly and windy day, I stood on the porch knocking on the door, left outside for what seemed like an eternity. When my aunt finally opened the door, I walked in with tears in my eyes. Then I saw her and my uncles sitting in a circle with their 40 ounces of beer, a pint of Seagram's 7 whiskey, and a glaze in their eyes that told me they were high.

"Why did you lock me out?" I asked my aunt as I walked through the living room.

My aunt was a hostile woman at times, and on that day, some of that hostility showed up. "I am grown! Don't question me," she replied. "Now get your ass in that room and watch some TV before I whoop yo' ass!"

That's something to tell your niece, isn't it? Especially one that you locked outside.

Tired of all the madness, I always wished my dysfunctional relatives would just move out. I thought maybe with them gone, we would at least have something. But when they finally left, I wished they were still there.

Even with my family drinking and doing drugs, they were there. I did not have to worry about me and my siblings being at home alone. I immediately regretted making that wish about them leaving. It was one I desperately wanted to take back.

♥

Though my siblings and I were not supposed to leave the house when we were at home alone, we would walk over to my step-aunt and cousins' house. I knew what rules to follow because my mom would always tell me not to open the door for anyone or go outside, but I did not like staying there alone. Most of the time, I would be afraid. I would be terrified of the thought of someone breaking in and me not knowing what to do or how to protect my siblings. During those days, we did not even have a phone, so I could not even call anyone if we needed help.

With my step-aunt being gone often, and out with my mom most times, being with my older cousins comforted me.

"Is Aunt Tiffany here?" I would ask my older cousin Theresa after walking over to my cousins' house, with my siblings in tow.

"No, she is gone," my cousin would reply.

"Well, can we stay over here with you until my mom gets back home?" My heart would always beat rapidly as I stood there, hoping the answer would be "yes".

"We're not supposed to let anyone in," my cousin would begin as I held my breath. "But yeah, you can stay. We are about to go down to the tunnels."

My cousins lived on a dead-end street with a creek next to their house that led to some tunnels down under. The tunnels were extremely dark and creepy, but we still went down there to see how far we could make it through. We treated them like some secret cave with hidden treasure. Though they were not anything spectacular, we enjoyed exploring the tunnels. It kept us kids occupied.

Those times used to be the highlight of my day, and I even looked forward to them until they ended abruptly one day. My mom had found an apartment, and we were moving . . . again. Now, we were moving to the north end of town and would no longer have anyone near us whom we knew or could rely on.

"Mom, why do we have to move again? I don't want to move down there," I pouted, trying to plead with her.

"Because I said so. I'm your momma; you not mine," she said, frustrated.

To me, we were not *just* moving; she was taking me away from another safe haven. When we moved down to the apartments, we were home alone more often, and we barely saw my mother. In my mother's absence, I graduated from handling big sister duties to fulfilling motherly responsibilities.

Though I did not know it back then, I became extremely depressed as the reality of not being able to live life as a normal preteen and having to take care of my brother and sister began sinking in. I would constantly have an attitude that I could not explain. At the time, I only knew I was short-tempered. My grades began slipping not only because I was tired and did not receive enough rest but also because I just did not care anymore.

While my mother was not at home, I was responsible for making sure Darnell and Precious ate, bathed, and prepared for bed. I was their safe haven during those days. Eventually, some new neighbors moved into the apartments right next door to us on the third floor, and we became really close to them. My siblings and I used to go either next door or downstairs all the time. My mom's ex-husband Bernard's cousin and his wife had moved downstairs, so they were like family to us. They looked out for us when we were home alone.

I was walking up the stairs with my siblings one day when I saw one of the kids from next door sitting on the stairs.

"What's up Kenya?" I asked her.

"Nothing much, girl, had to come out here and do my homework because I am tired of the BS in there."

Though I could not make out their words, I could hear what sounded like someone arguing inside Kenya's apartment.

She continued, "I wish they would just leave. I would prefer to be home alone like you rather than deal with their stuff."

I looked at Kenya in bewilderment as I contemplated what she said. *She would rather be home alone, and I would rather have my mom at home.* It amazed me how people could look at one another and secretly wish they could trade places.

"Girl, you can come inside if you want to do your homework, or at least until they stop arguing," I offered. She quickly gathered her things, taking me up on my offer.

Everything seemed cool as I sat on the floor talking to Kenya that evening. She had gone back home, but we both had our front doors open and were sitting in the hallway next to them. We were laughing and joking when a knock at my back door interrupted me mid-sentence. I told Kenya to hold on and walked to the back door to see who was knocking.

"Where is your mother at?" a white woman asked when I answered the door.

"She's not here." I held the door partially open so that the woman could not see inside.

"I am Cindy, and I am with DCFS. We have complaints of you and your siblings being left alone a lot."

Confused and trembling, I told the woman, "We are not here alone."

Leaving the door slightly ajar, I ran downstairs and told our stepcousin's wife that a white woman was upstairs and she was with DCFS.

"I'm scared; are they going to take us?" I asked her frantically.

"No, let's go," she said.

We raced back upstairs, my heart pounding in my chest.

"Hello, my name is Pam, and I watch these kids. They are never here alone. I stay downstairs and their mom pays me to keep an eye on them. I had to run downstairs to check on something," Pam told the DCFS lady.

"We had an anonymous call come through with a complaint saying these kids are here alone all day every day," Cindy told Pam.

"That's not the case at all, and I'm not sure why someone would say that," Pam lied.

Even though Cindy eventually left with no findings, she seemed very hesitant to leave. I could see her eyes searching the place, and she would look from me to Pam with an expression on her face that said, "I know you two are lying." It was a scary moment for me because I did not know what would happen. I did not know if we would be taken away, or if we would be split up.

I closed the back door as Cindy left, and as I turned to walk away from the door, Kenya burst through the front door.

"Girl, are you okay? Who was that?" she asked.

"Some woman from DCFS," I responded.

Normally, I did not tell our business, but Kenya was one of my best friends, so I did not have any problems telling her about Cindy. We had talked about so much stuff before, so I felt comfortable telling her the truth.

"I didn't know what to do. I was scared for you," she replied.

I then told her, "We are going to be okay," unsure if we would be.

As several scenarios played in my mind, Kenya continued talking. "Girl, I heard my mom tell my stepdad one day that someone needs to call DCFS because it's a shame that you guys are always home alone."

I loved Kenya, but now was not the time for her extra commentary, so I told her again, "We are going to be okay, and I think it's time for you to go home."

Just like Cindy, she hesitated to leave but eventually walked back across the hall.

Even after Kenya left, I could not get what she had just said, nor the event that had taken place with DCFS, out of my head. My mind raced at full speed.

I went looking for Pam after taking a moment to regroup.

"I truly do appreciate you coming up here and lying to that lady for us," I said as I fiddled with my hands. "Thank you for caring and standing up for us. I am forever grateful," I expressed to Pam, holding back the tears.

Pam said, "You listen here, I did not lie to that lady. As long as I am home, you and your siblings will never be here alone. I will always look after you guys, and you are always welcome downstairs."

As the tears began to fall, I thanked Pam again and hugged her. I nearly melted in her arms, unsure of how long it had been since I felt my mother's embrace. When we released each other, Pam started walking toward the back door to leave and said, "Now lock this door behind me and don't answer this door no more tonight."

I did what she said and prepared myself and my siblings for bed.

The next day, I got up and peeped into my mom's bedroom as she lay in bed, still asleep. I tiptoed into her room and woke her up to tell her about what had happened the night before.

"That was Bernard that called on me," she said, a sternness to her voice.

"How do you know?" I asked. "Kenya said her mom said—"

My mom cut me off and said, "I told you it was Bernard that called on me."

I looked at her crazily, but I knew better than to challenge my mom. So I just left it alone.

And that was the end of the whole ordeal. Thankfully, we never heard anything else from Cindy, and it was all thanks to Pam.

♥

"Mom, I really don't like this school. I'm having problems here, and I'm tired of crying because I'm so unhappy there. Every day is an issue, and I can't take it anymore," I expressed to my mom one day as we sat outside on our back stairs.

It was a lovely day outside. The sun was shining, and my mom was sitting still, which did not happen often, so I had to take this opportunity to talk to her about how I was feeling.

"What's the problem?" she questioned as she brushed her hair.

"The kids keep picking with me," I replied.

"Just ignore them," she said, as if solving my problem were that simple.

"Ignoring them doesn't work. They still keep picking on me and talking about me. I don't want to go to that school anymore. Can I please go stay with Aunt Angel and Uncle Clark?"

"No," my mom replied, with no hesitation at all.

Refusing to accept no for an answer, I begged and pleaded for days and even weeks before my mom allowed me to stay with my aunt and uncle. A couple of months later, August 1995 to be exact, I moved in with my aunt and uncle at the start of my 7th grade year. I was excited about the change, but I wondered how my mom actually felt about it. I knew Precious was too young to understand and Darnell was such a momma's boy that he probably did not care, but I wondered if my mom would miss me or even care that I was gone.

A drastic change from the previous school year, I loved my new school. I finally made true friends. I participated in extracurricular activities and received invitations to birthday parties, dances, and movies, and I was feeling the way every twelve-year-old girl should feel. Everything was perfect, except for my home life.

At home, it seemed as if Aunt Angel did not truly want me there. Yes, I had more freedom while living there, but her vibe told me she did not want me there, and I felt it every time I was in the same room with her.

"I got you some new shoes for your track meet on Thursday," Uncle Clark told me once.

As I opened my mouth to say thank you to my uncle, Aunt Angel interrupted me. "Why did you buy her shoes? She has some shoes to wear. You always give her money and buy her stuff," she complained.

Aunt Angel's comments made me feel like she was either jealous or angry because Uncle Clark was trying to be there for me as a father figure, and she did not like it. Instead of responding, I walked into my room and shut the door. I lay in bed and cried because it hurt to feel unwanted by my family. I thought living with them would give me a better chance at life, but it just added to the pain and depression I felt inside.

"After the school year is up, you will be going back to stay with your mom," Aunt Angel said after coming into my room to deliver the final blow.

"Okay," I replied, refusing to let my hurt show.

I did not have the energy to beg her to stay. If she did not want me there, then I would just leave. With me being back at home with my mom, at least I would not have to deal with the side remarks, the sideways glances, and the negative energy I received from my aunt. I would have rather been with my mother and become a surrogate parent again than deal with all the unnecessary drama.

Chapter 5

In 1996, I moved back home with my mom and my new stepdad, Bobby. Now thirteen years old, I continued attending the same school as before, but Darnell and I had to wake up early in the morning to catch a public bus to get to school. One morning, I found myself knocking on my mother's bedroom door at 6:30 am, trying to wake her and convince her to take us to school because we had missed the city bus.

The bus would come at 6:15 am, and it would go downtown to the bus lineup. From there, we would have to transfer to another bus to get to our school on time. Because the bus ride would be a long one, I would close my eyes and take a little nap. Sometimes I could not sleep because of all the commotion on the bus. After the bus came to a stop one morning, an older white gentleman attempted to get on but did not have any money. Going from zero to a hundred, the man started yelling, calling the bus driver all kinds of names. The bus driver tried to convince the man to stop yelling or she would have to call the police. Because of the altercation, the bus was late getting down to the lineup, which made us late for school, as usual.

"Mom, can you please take us to school?" I asked, hoping to make it to school on time that day. "We missed the bus."

"Stop knocking on my door! You better get to walking or ride your bike because I'm not getting up," she spat. "You should've had your butt up in time to catch that bus."

I shook my head because I could not believe what my mom was saying. She actually expected us to walk five miles, if not more, to school, and we lived all the way on the south end of town. Unfortunately, my mother said this all the time when we missed the bus or did not have another ride to school. Sometimes my brother and I even had to take turns riding each other on a bike just to get to school. My mother's attitude toward the situation upset me even more because it was as if she did not care about her own children's well-being. Anything could have happened to us, but I guess her sleep mattered more.

♥

My resentment toward my mom and my stepdad grew more and more each day. The major issue I had with my stepdad was that he came in with two kids of his own, for whom I now had to be responsible. And with more responsibilities came more rules. My stepdad would come in barking orders, and it pissed me off because I felt like I was the one who had been in charge, and in he walked dishing out his stuff. The more my mom and stepdad tried to make me follow their rules, the more I acted out. I got so fed up with their little "family" that I was ready to bail out on all of them. I grew tired of feeling like a maid, the help that never got paid for her services.

When will enough be enough? I often wondered. *How long do I have to feel like the black sheep?*

"Can I go over to Tish's house?" I asked my stepdad one day.

"No, you are to stay in this house," he ordered.

My face turned blood red as heat rushed through my body. I was livid. They did not understand I was tired of sitting in the house every day with *their* kids and wanted to hang out with my cousin for a while. I just wanted a little break. Determined to break free from their grasp, I decided to take matters into my own hands.

I waited for my stepdad to fall asleep, and then I called my cousin Tish to meet me eight blocks from my house, which was halfway. When the time was right, I boldly walked out the front door. My mom was at work, and I was not about to sit in that house any longer with people who irritated me so badly.

Tish and I walked to a couple of our friends' houses and hung out for a while. As night fell, we headed back to my house.

Once I approached the door, I discovered all the doors were locked. I thought to myself, *Where will we go*? Even though I knew I was wrong for leaving, I was not in the mood to hear Bobby's mouth. I peeped through the windows and spotted my siblings sitting there, so I knocked on the window and asked them to open the door. They all ignored me except for my little stepbrother, Jeffrey.

I knocked on the window again. "Jeffrey, come open the door! Let me in," I pleaded with him.

"Dad said we can't open the door for you," he yelled out.

I became furious, but not because of Jeffrey; he was only four years old. I was mad at Bobby for locking me out of the house and leaving me outside. Though it was already dark and getting later by the minute, I pretended as if it did not faze me.

My cousin Tish and I left the house and headed to hers. I sat on the porch with my cousin until my mom got off and came to pick me up. I thought my mom was going to jump down my throat, but surprisingly, she didn't. When my mother pulled up to my cousin's house, I stepped off the porch and hopped into the yellow and white pickup truck, which I hated, by the way. I put my seat belt on and turned my head to look at my mom. She was quiet and looked so tired. I could tell she had a long day at work.

Out of nowhere, she said, "You know you shouldn't have left the house, and you need to apologize when we get home."

I did not respond to my mom because there was no way I was going to apologize to Bobby. I thought to myself, *This lady has lost her mind*. There was no way in hell I was going to bow down to him. I knew my mom was just trying to keep the peace, but I wondered if she understood why I decided to sneak out.

As soon as we walked into the house, Bobby started going in on me.

"I told you not to leave this house, and as soon as I go to sleep, you take your grown ass and leave!" he shouted.

The whole time I just looked at him and rolled my eyes because I was so annoyed. I balled up my fists and mugged him as he continued to yell.

"Oh, so you think you bad? Do you want to fight?"

I stood there quietly and watched him as he moved the coffee table to the side and stood in the middle of the floor, looking at me like I was some dude on the streets.

"Bring yo' ass since you think you bad!"

I stood there as still as a rock, just glaring at him.

Then Bobby got in my face and pushed me in my chest while yelling, "You are going to follow my rules while you are in my house!"

"I don't have to listen to you; you are not my dad," I yelled back. I looked over at my mom and demanded, "I want to go live with my dad!"

My mom looked at me and replied, "No, you are staying here."

Sadness quickly washed over my face. "But I'm not happy. I don't want to be here," I said, my voice nearly cracking.

"She wants to go, let her go," my stepdad interjected.

Not even a second later, I hurried to the phone and called my real dad, Oliver. About two hours later, Oliver came down to the house.

"I want to go with you and live with you at your house," I told him.

He hesitated. "I think you need to stay here with your mom and Bobby," Oliver said, looking over at them as he finished his statement.

My heart shattered as soon as the words left his lips. Though I could hear Oliver, my jumbled thoughts began drowning him out. There I was crying and explaining to my dad that I was unhappy and wanted to live with him, and he was trying to convince me to stay where I was. Those feelings of rejection rushed in like a tidal wave. It seemed as if my dad did not want me at his house. That was the most crushing feeling ever, a child out in the world feeling like both a motherless and a fatherless child. Tears from wanting to escape the unfair treatment from my mom and stepdad escalated to tears from feeling like my dad did not want to take me in, his own daughter. In that hurtful moment, I decided to wash my hands with everyone. No one had protected me before, and they still refused to protect me now.

♥

Four months later, my fourteenth birthday rolled around on February 14th. I did not know if it was because of Valentine's Day or if something else was in the air, but my stepdad surprised me that morning. I had just finished getting dressed and was standing in the bathroom mirror, putting my hair in a ponytail, when he walked up to the door.

"Happy Birthday," he said.

"Thank you," I replied dryly.

"How would you feel if I said you can drive yourself to school today?" he asked.

"Really?" He had my full attention then. "That would be awesome!"

"Well, today is your lucky day. I am going to trust you and allow you to drive to school today for your birthday."

My eyes grew wide, and I smiled so hard. "Are you serious?"

"Yes," he replied with a smile.

"Thank you, thank you." I gave him a big hug. He was actually letting me drive his silver '93 Cadillac Deville to school.

I felt like I was on top of the world, and I knew I was going to be envied by all my peers. I could just see the surprised looks on their faces when I pulled up in the

Caddy. Just the thought of all eyes being on me filled me with excitement.

Of course, no child should be unsupervised behind the wheel of a car, but that gesture made me appreciate Bobby a little more because it showed his trust in me and his effort to make my day special. I honestly thought we were headed in the right direction, building a genuine bond.

While I do not know if the blow-up between me and Bobby had shifted our family dynamic, I do know things had definitely changed. Our home life was not as hectic anymore, and I was thriving at school. We finally had the structure and stability we had been craving, until my stepdad made me and Darnell transfer to a school in our district. Another bombshell. It felt as if someone had aimed a cannon at my stomach and let it rip. *I can't believe this is happening to me . . . and in the middle of my eighth-grade year*, I thought.

When I first heard the news, all I could think about was not being able to share the same stage with my friends at graduation. I would have rather walked to school every day instead of transferring schools. I know it made no sense, but I would have done anything to stay at school with my friends.

Shortly after I got the news, I walked over to my friend Tam's house after school one day. As we were walking, I told her, "Tam, my mom and Bobby are making me and my brother transfer schools."

"What? Why?" she asked, her eyes searching for answers.

"Because they want to ruin my life." I fought back the tears. "I don't want to go down there to that school. I'm going to be down there by myself."

"Just because we will be at different schools doesn't mean we won't be hanging out or still be friends," she assured me.

We embraced, and then I smiled. "Thank you," I said.

Even though that hug relieved me of my concerns at the moment, I still fought for a chance to stay at school with my friends. Despite my begging and pleading, my plea remained unheard. I was on my way to another school.

On the first day, my face said it all. Though I wanted to keep a positive attitude, I walked into my new school with my guard up because I did not know those people and I was not in the mood to make new friends. The school was a fairly large school that looked kind of old and a little deadly. It reminded me of a haunted school I had seen once on TV. Some people seemed genuine and kind, and then some seemed like stuck-up snobs. Needless to say, it took a while for me to warm up to my new surroundings.

"Would you like to join the basketball team?" the basketball coach asked me one day after watching me shooting around during gym class.

"I'm in eighth grade, and the season started, so I can't," I replied, not knowing what to say because her interest caught me by surprise. Honestly, I did not want to play for the school because I would be playing against my crew. I did not want to feel like a traitor.

"Well, I am the coach, and if you are interested, be at practice this afternoon after school," she smirked. The expression on her face saying, "You've got this."

Curious about what the basketball team had to offer, I went to practice, fully aware that the coach already knew I would. Surprisingly, it was not what I expected. I thought the practice would be more difficult because my previous coach did not play any games, but it was pretty chill. I also thought I would have to do a tryout session, but I didn't. On that same day, the coach told me I was on the team, and that I had to maintain good grades to stay on it.

I must admit, it was pretty exciting to attend a new school and get on the basketball team when the season had already started. Excited, I went home and immediately told my parents the good news. Not only did I get on the team, but I would also start in a few games.

Being on the team helped me warm up to my peers, Zora in particular. She was always sweet and kind to me. While she might not have known it, her kindness made me feel more accepted, like I could belong there.

♥

Even though I met some friends, I also had some enemies. These girls had no reason not to like me, but I would hear the whispers in the hallways and in the classrooms. "She thinks she is too cute" echoed the loudest because I heard it all the time. Hearing it once was more than enough to make me want to leave the school, so just imagine how it felt to hear it every day. How could I think I was too cute when so much had been taken from me? When some days I wished I could live a completely different life? They had no idea just how much I carried inside.

One day, a loud knock at the door disturbed me and my cousin Tish from watching TV. We were sitting in the TV room watching the movie *Friday*, just about to see the fight go down between Craig and Deebo. Ironically, I opened the door to find about five people standing in my yard. When I spotted someone hiding behind the tree, I stepped outside onto the porch. The sun was shining in my eyes, nearly blinding me, and I could feel the mild heat on my skin. The pounding in my chest let me know things were about to get hotter.

"Come outside," one girl yelled.

"I'm outside," I shouted back, rolling my neck with each word.

The same girl said, "Come to the yard. I want to fight you!"

"Oh, okay, hold on for a second." I sprinted back into the house and told Tish, "Girl, get up and put your shoes on. There's some people out in the yard that want to fight me, and I'm going out there."

Without hesitation, Tish reached for her shoes, and I followed suit. Then I put my hair in a quick ponytail. I was not a fighter, but I definitely was not about to let anyone punk me at my own house. There were rules to this, and one was that you did not show up at anyone's house to fight and think you were going to get away with it. I was not worried because I knew I was not going down with my cousin by my side; she would not let me get jumped. I had no fear, none whatsoever.

As we were inches away from the door, my mom stopped us. "What are y'all doing?"

"It's some kids out there that came over here to fight me, so we are about to go outside and fight them." Clearly, I was amped up and ready to go. I did not even think about downplaying what was happening in front of my mom.

"You are not taking your ass out nowhere to fight nobody; get yo' ass back in this house!" My mom's high-pitched voice let me know she meant business.

Tish and I exchanged glances, and I knew we were on the same page. I pleaded with my mom to let us go out there, but she was not having it. She darted out the door.

"Y'all can get your bad asses out my door with that fighting shit! You're not about to fight nobody over here, so get out my yard right now!"

The disappointment immediately swept over my face because I wanted to let them know I was not afraid of them. I then wondered how my mom could interfere with this fight but not the fight I had been fighting ever since I was five years old. Once again, someone had taken my choice away from me, so much so that I questioned if I ever had one.

Once my mom disappeared into the back room to finish watching TV, my cousin and I plotted to sneak outside to finish what those other girls had started. As soon as my mom was not paying attention, we snuck around the corner to the main girl's house, but no one was outside. We walked that route at least five times that day, but we ended the night by returning home to watch TV. Even though the TV was on, all I could think about was those girls.

When my stepdad came home, he was also upset that my mom did not let me go out there to fight. I never knew why. But in the midst of that confusion, one positive thing did happen: I was returning to my old school to graduate with my friends.

Chapter 6

Summer 1997 had begun, and I was excited to be out of middle school. While the thought of being a freshman terrified me because high school was a different ball game, I was ready to enjoy every bit of the summer.

When my older cousin Shauna moved back home from college, I moved back in with Aunt Angel and Uncle Clark. Shauna took me under her wing and looked out for me. Even though I was her little cousin, she treated me like I was her little sister. Wherever she went, I was there with her. She would take me shopping, bowling, and to the movies. Sometimes we would climb into my uncle's Bronco and ride around town just to get out of the house.

I ended the summer by taking a two-week trip with my cousins, aunts, and uncles. We began the trip in Illinois and traveled to Mississippi for our family reunion. My uncles and aunts occupied the van, while my cousins Shauna, Karlos, Jesse, and I rode in my aunt's white Roadmaster. During the car ride, I often drifted off, thinking about how relaxing it was to be in the car with my family, on the road, and getting out of Illinois. When I was not drifting off, my cousins and I would sit there listening and rapping along to Master P and TRU. In between listening to music, we would talk about everything from school to the dangers of being on the road at night, and the scary movies where most of those scenes occurred.

Throughout the twelve-hour trip to Mississippi, I gazed out the window, staring at all the trees and cars. I would even look at people's license plates to see where they were from, wondering what it would be like to live in their city.

We finally arrived in Corinth, Mississippi on a Thursday night and planned to stay until that Sunday morning. We pulled up at the hotel and immediately noticed its name: The Crossroads Hotel. When we noticed the sign, my cousins and I burst out laughing. My cousin Jesse got out of the car dancing and singing "Tha Crossroads" by Bone Thugs-N-Harmony. Not missing a beat, we all got out of the car and joined in with him.

What I remember most about Mississippi is that it was scorching hot, and the bugs were huge. Despite the discomfort, I enjoyed my time down there because I met several family members I had never met before.

Next up on our trip was the Lake of the Ozarks in Arkansas. We had rented a house on the lake, and it was such a peaceful place. Arkansas differed slightly from Mississippi because it seemed to have plenty of nature and fishing. You could hear the sounds of the water, the birds, and even the bugs. You could have a clear mind out there. Just being one with nature.

I loved fishing when we visited the lake, but I refused to put the worm on the hook, or to take the fish off the hook. We even had contests for who caught the most or the biggest fish. My cousin Karlos won the contest for the biggest fish, and I won for the most fish, even though my cousins were a little upset because they had to help me bait my hook. In my eyes, the time we spent there was like a breath of fresh air.

After leaving Arkansas, we arrived in Oakdale, Louisiana for my Uncle Clark's family reunion. It was a very small town that shut down super early. It looked like a black Mayberry, the fictional town in *The Andy Griffith Show*. Even though I believed Mayberry might have been bigger, I noticed more people in Oakdale than I did on the show.

♥

In the fall of 1997, I began high school, class of 2001. I started the school year off living with my grandmother because she lived within the district of the school I wanted to attend. My family still lived on the south end.

By this time, I hung out more with my younger sister, Brandi. Brandi was my dad's other daughter. Not only was she my sister on my dad's side, but she was also my second cousin on my mom's side. Yes, my mom and her mom were first cousins. Surprisingly, there was no bad blood between them about the situation, and if there ever was, they never showed it.

Hanging out with Brandi brought so much joy into my life. I loved her so much, and we always had fun together. Our relationship played a huge part in me walking into high school with so much more confidence. Every week, my cousin Shauna would style my hair, and she never charged me. Brandi's mom, Brittney, would get boxes of clothes fresh off the truck and let us pick the items we wanted before she sold the rest. I must say, I looked good, and I felt even better.

I would stay at Brandi's house almost every weekend. It was my personal getaway. Brandi's mom was pretty laid back, and she was not too strict. She would allow us to hang out on the porch late at night, walk to the store by ourselves, and have company over. I enjoyed being down there with them because my parents did not allow me to have that kind of freedom at home.

Brittney dated a man named Gary, whose right eye appeared to be on the lazy side. Brandi and I would lie awake at night and talk about him whenever he made us mad. We would crack so many jokes about him. I would always tell Brandi that his eye was going to jump down and chase us around the house. Horrible, I know.

Though we did not like Gary, his friend Shaun would come around often, and he became our surrogate uncle. He would pick us up and take us for rides, dropping us off at the bowling alley on Friday nights and picking us up after we finished bowling. He really took care of us, which was more than we could say about Gary, or Brittney's ex-boyfriend Sam, who was married. The only thing Sam did was stop us from eating pork, being that he was a Muslim.

Late one afternoon, people were still outside, enjoying the summer day. Brandi and I parked ourselves in the living room by the front door, watching people pass by the house.

"Why is Sam and his crew outside, sitting in the church parking lot?" I asked Brandi, taking a bite of my hot pickle.

"I don't know," she said, sipping on her Kool-Aid. Brandi then hurried into the house to let Brittney know her ex-boyfriend and his crew were posted up outside. Brandi came back with her mom in tow.

Brittney popped her lips. "They look so stupid sitting over there."

As I wondered why they would even come down there when Sam and Brittney were not even together anymore, Brandi interrupted my thoughts.

"Are they here to fight Gary?" Brandi asked her mom.

"I hope not," Brittney said.

Just minutes later, Sam and his crew rushed across the street to Brittney's house to start trouble with Gary. Gary heard the commotion and stormed out onto the porch.

"Y'all better get from in front of this house with y'all bullshit," Gary yelled out.

Sam and his crew inched closer, and within a split second, someone had hit Gary.

"Stop, get off him!" Brittney screamed frantically.

I could not believe my eyes. They were jumping Gary right in front of us. Brandi rushed off, to where I do not know, but she flew by like a bat out of hell. I could still hear her mother yelling over the commotion.

"Stop! Stop!"

I searched my surroundings to see if I could find anything to give to Brittney. Luckily, I rushed over to the neighbor's yard and found a pole. I handed the pole to Brittney so that she could knock Sam in the head, but to my surprise, she didn't. She just continued to scream.

"Get off him! I'm calling the police!"

Instantly, Sam and his crew stopped fighting and then piled into their cars and left. We could hear the tires screeching as they sped around the corner. I always thought it was funny how people scattered like roaches at the mention of the police.

Trying to process what had just happened, I sat on the porch to gather my thoughts and slow my breathing. I turned to see Brandi sprinting around the corner.

"Where did you go?" I asked Brandi.

"Shoot, I went to go get help. Gary needed some help," she said, laughing and out of breath.

"Girl, you missed the whole fight," I teased.

"What happened?" she asked anxiously.

We sat on the porch for hours, laughing and gossiping about the events that had transpired. The funniest part of it all was seeing Brittney standing there with that pole panicking, not knowing what to do. Her facial expression was priceless. There was never a dull moment at Brandi's house.

♥

As the afternoon slipped into the evening, Brandi and I would sit on the porch, bored with watching the cars drive by and people walk down the street. We often wondered what we could do to entertain ourselves.

"We should call Shaun and see if he could drop us off at the movies tonight," I told Brandi one day.

"Ooh, yes," Brandi replied.

"Let's ask Brittney if we can go tonight," I said.

"You ask her because she's probably going to say no," Brandi said.

"Well, come on." I knew I was being used, but at least I would be getting something out of it, too.

"Brittney, can Brandi and I go to the movies tonight?" I asked Brittney with a plea in my eyes. "Shaun said he would take us."

"Not tonight because I am going out, but y'all can tomorrow night," she replied. "I do want y'all to go down to the store and get me a cup of ice while I get dressed."

We nodded and reluctantly headed toward the door.

"Y'all go and come right back. Don't be down there messing around," she called after us.

We loved to walk down to the store because there was always something going on down there, and we would surely run into people we knew. Sometimes we would get so caught up in talking and playing around that we would lose track of the time.

In the middle of our walk to the store, Brandi and I noticed a guy from the area walking toward us. We knew him well. His little sister was a friend of ours, and he was always on the block. Before he could get close to us, two boys ran up and shot him. It happened before I could even blink. There we were, not even fifty feet away, and we witnessed our friend getting shot.

My heart pounded, and my legs trembled. I grabbed my sister's hand, but we were too scared to even move. We were completely stuck in place. I had never seen anyone get shot before, and I could not believe it had happened right in front of me.

The two shooters immediately ran off, and a few other guys rushed over to help our friend.

"Get out of here," one of them yelled.

Still holding hands, Brandi and I ran back to the house and fell through the front door, jabbering to Brittney about what had just happened. Though we did not stick around to see what happened to our friend, we eventually found out he was taken to the hospital.

It was definitely a night I would never forget. I sat up most of the night, lying there in the dark, staring up at the ceiling. When I tried to fall asleep, I would toss and turn, wondering how I could erase the images from that day out of my head.

♥

Even though it seemed as if so much drama went down around Brandi's house, I still loved being with her. I loved not having to be stuck at home watching my siblings. While Brandi and I had to watch Brandi's siblings sometimes, we would be *together*, and not stuck in the house.

The only time I was not at Brandi's house was when I was at my grandma's house for school. In my grandma's apartment, I would have to walk through her bedroom to get to the living room. On this one particular night, Brandi had come over to stay with me. Instead of staying in the bedroom, we decided to go into the living room to watch TV because my room did not have one. We also knew we would have access to the front porch. As we opened my grandma's door to walk to the living room, our eyes grew wide as we spotted her on top of her boyfriend having sex. We had to keep going to get to the TV, so we ran through the room and flopped down on the couch, both tickled and disgusted at the same time.

"Oh my gosh, I can't believe Aunt Christy was on top of that man riding him," Brandi could barely talk through her laughter. "Keren, I think my eyes are burning."

I laughed so hard that my stomach was hurting and tears were coming from my eyes.

"Mine, too! I don't think I can ever shake that thought."

Though that incident was a humorous one, Grandma's rendezvous made me not want to stay home on the weekends anymore. I was not that experienced in the sex department to know exactly what was happening, but I knew I could not bear the thought of seeing my grandmother like that again. With Thanksgiving approaching, I decided to spend the holiday break with Brandi, after receiving my grandmother's approval, of course.

When Brittney left to make a run to the grocery store, we put the kids' coats on to walk down to the store to get some junk food. As we walked back home from the store, Brandi's little sister, Alexis, darted out into the street. A car sped down the street and hit Alexis. I watched in horror as she, a little six-year-old girl, lay in the street. I took off running toward her, and Brandi chased after the car as the person kept going. How heartless! He did not even stop to see if she was okay, or even alive.

I rushed over to Alexis and scooped her into my arms. Scared out of my mind, I held her so close to me that I drenched her with my tears. Brandi returned huffing and puffing because she could no longer keep up with the car, which was impossible for her to do. She was only thirteen years old, standing about 5'5" with a small body frame. I do not even remember what she said, if she said anything. The only thing I remember is carrying Alexis home and laying her fragile body on the couch. Brandi then called her mom, barely able to tell her what had just happened. After hearing the news, Brittney rushed home to take Alexis to the emergency room.

The next day was Thanksgiving, but there was no celebration. Brittney and Alexis were still at the hospital. Brandi, her two little brothers, and I were at the house alone, eating cereal for dinner, until my mom came over later that night with plates of food. Even though it was kind of depressing because we were home alone on Thanksgiving, it was still cool because we were together. I missed my family a little, but being that I felt like the black sheep, it comforted me more to be near my sister.

Brittney and Alexis finally came home two days later. Alexis had suffered a broken leg, and she had to have a cast put on it. Brittney's sister Stephanie also showed up that night, and she said she had talked to the guy who had hit Alexis. She had seen him inside the corner store and knew exactly who he was because we had told her about him.

"Wake will be coming over tonight, and I want y'all to hide in my room and listen, and when he admits to hitting Alexis, or if anything happens, call the police," she told us.

Brandi and I agreed to do as Brittney said. Even though we were hesitant, we knew we had little choice in the matter.

Three hours had passed, and we were all sitting in the living room, laughing and joking around when a knock sounded at the door. Brandi and I looked at each other and took off running to Brittney's room, with Brandi snatching the cordless phone along the way. We turned off the light to blend in with the dark.

Steph went to the door. "Who is it?" she asked.

I heard a deep voice say, "It's Wake."

My heart started pounding, and my hands began sweating.

Brandi whispered to me, "Girl, I am so scared."

I chuckled nervously and then replied, "Me, too."

We could hear them talking while we were standing close to the door, peeping into the living room.

"I don't recall hitting her," Wake said, seeming as if he were becoming agitated. I prayed the situation would not escalate to anything more than them just talking.

"I'm just letting you know if you do, you will be going to jail," Brittney said sternly.

Suddenly, the door opened and then closed. Brandi and I peeped into the room, and Brittney told us we could come out because Wake was gone. We darted out of the room and plopped down on the couch.

"He didn't admit to anything," Brittney informed us. "He will get his, though. He will pay." Hearing those words chilled my soul.

As traumatic as it was, even the hit-and-run did not stop me from going to Brittney's house. That type of action brought a sense of excitement to my life that I did not want to let go.

♥

Goodness, I am bored, I thought to myself. I sat on the porch with the smell of barbecue filling my nose. I could hear kids playing their games, and the sirens from police cars racing down the street.

"Brittney, can I walk down to the store?" I asked.

"Can you take us with you?" Alexis and Gill, one of Brandi's little brothers, asked just as Brittney opened her mouth to speak.

I did not want to take them because they were so young, and I would have to walk slowly and hold their hands. After enduring only a few seconds of their whining, I gave in.

Walking down the street as we headed toward the store, I noticed one of the girls who had shown up at my mother's house. She and her little crew were following us.

"Here we are. We can fight now," I heard the girl say.

"I'm not scared of you," I yelled back. "We sure can as soon as I take my little brother and sister to the store."

I hurried along but looked back a time or two because they were walking behind me. Once we entered the store, I turned to Alexis and Gill.

"Get your stuff, but hurry up so I can get y'all back home before these people start some mess."

Alexis and Gill obeyed, both of them wearing confused looks on their faces.

I allowed them to get their candy, but I stood at the counter looking out the glass door in front of the store to keep my eyes on the enemy. Only when Alexis and Gill walked up to the counter did I look away.

"Are y'all ready?"

"Yes," they replied simultaneously.

I paid for their candy, and I grabbed their hands, telling them to come on and walk fast. The group was still outside, and I walked right past them. They followed close behind.

"I can't wait to kick your ass," the enemy taunted.

"Yeah, I would love to see that," I shot back.

Then I heard someone call out, "Hey, Keren!"

I noticed a guy from the block, whom I was cool with, posted up with two other guys.

"What's up?" I said, still walking.

"Stop for a minute and let me talk to you," he said.

"Not right now. I have to get them home so I can fight the girl that's following behind me."

"Who?" he responded.

"That crowd behind me." I looked over my shoulder.

His eyes cut past me as he looked behind me. "Aw, hell naw! That's not about to happen." He shifted his gaze back to me. "Look, we are not about to let them jump you. Come on."

I started walking again, and the three homeboys began walking with me, making sure I got home with no problems.

"Y'all might as well go on about your business because y'all not about to jump her," one of the homeboys told the enemy.

I noticed the crew had stopped at a yellow and red house, but I continued walking down the street, getting closer to Brandi's house.

"Gone to the house. I will get with you later. Okay," my homeboy told me.

"Okay. Definitely."

Once Alexis and Gill were safely in the house, I hurried to the bathroom to grab a blade and put it in my mouth.

"What's wrong?" Brandi and Brittney asked in unison.

I spoke so fast that I could hardly catch my breath. "Tonya and them just called themselves wanting to jump me as I walked to the store. They followed me all the way to the store and back home. C.M., Jack, and John walked us home to make sure they didn't jump me."

Without hesitation, Brandi ran into the bathroom and grabbed a blade, too, and we flew out the door.

We stood on the porch waiting for the group to come around the corner, but Brittney met us outside.

"What are y'all doing?"

"We are about to walk around the corner and see if they are still there," I said.

"You don't go looking for them. If they want problems, then they will come around here. If they come around here, and then the police come, y'all won't get in trouble because they came to y'all house."

Of course, I thought that was bullshit because I wanted to fight the girl so badly. I was tired of her trying to pick on me, but I understood what Brittney was trying to tell us. I never looked at it from her point of view. It made total sense.

Still, Brandi and I sat on the porch waiting for over two hours, but the girls never came around the corner. I was thankful they did not show up because I was at a point where I knew I was going to cut one of the girls in their crew. And I knew if I cut one of them, then I could have hurt them badly, or even killed them. Just the thought of being a juvenile delinquent frightened me. I had heard so many horror stories and knew I would have to fight just about every day for my survival. I still remembered the pain of leaving my Uncle Skeeter behind as we left the prison and did not want my family to experience that same pain. Even though I never told her, I was so grateful Brittney kept us on the porch that day.

Chapter 7

Valentine's Day 1998 . . . I could not believe I was fifteen years old. Only three more years of being a minor. I was extra excited about this birthday because not only was I having my friends over to spend the night, but my mom and stepdad were also taking me and my friends to Indiana to celebrate my birthday with my cousins.

On the night before my birthday, I sat in the sitting room with my parents, gushing about how I could not wait to get out of Illinois the next day. I was thanking them for taking me out of town when we heard a knock on the door.

"Who is it?" my mom asked as she stood next to the door, waiting to hear who would respond.

"It's Tonya," the voice on the other side of the door said.

Tonya was one of my best friends from school, and we would take turns staying at each other's houses. I was ecstatic that she was spending my birthday weekend with me. My other friend, Betty, who we called Bee, came over, too.

"So, what do you guys want to do?" my stepdad asked as we all sat around chatting.

"Can we have some of y'all drinks?" I asked my parents, trying to look as innocent as possible.

They were drinking some E&J Brandy; everyone used to call it Erk and Jerk. Though they hesitated at first, they agreed to let us drink with them. Ironically, they preferred for us to have a drink with them instead of sneaking around and drinking with people who did not have our best interest at heart.

That night was one for the books. My friends and I had drinks with my parents, sang karaoke, and ate pizza. Surprisingly, my parents threw up from all the liquor, not us. It was one of the best birthdays ever, and it was not over yet.

When we woke up the next day, the aroma of bacon filled the house; my mom was in the kitchen cooking. Though the sun was shining, it was freezing. I guess all the alcohol from the night before made me forget it was February.

"Y'all get up and start getting into motion so y'all can eat and we can get on the road and head out to Indiana," my mom said as she flipped the bacon.

"Okay, when are we leaving?" I asked.

"I want to be on the road by two," she responded.

"Did Brandi call? Is she able to go with us?" I asked, anticipating my mom's answer. Of course, I wanted my sister to go with me.

"Yes, she called; she said Brittney won't let her go. She has to help her mom with the kids, but she wants you to have fun and to call her."

My mom's words crushed me. I was upset because this trip was supposed to be an exciting time for me, but I could not bring my sister with me. While I was not upset with Brandi, I was upset with Brittney for not allowing her to go. I could not understand why she could not watch her own kids. I did not understand why parents thought it was the oldest child's responsibility to care for the younger kids. They were not our kids, so why did we have to miss out on things because of *their* kids? Brandi not being able to join me on my birthday trip definitely struck a nerve. I was probably being selfish, but I did not care because it was my birthday and I could be mad if I wanted to. I wanted my sister right beside me, and she wasn't there.

Even though Brandi could not go on the trip, I still had my other two friends with me. I refused to let Brandi's absence, or Brittney's parenting, ruin our trip. So I got over it pretty quickly. After a few minutes of pouting and rolling my eyes, I was back on track. I was grateful to have my friends by my side, and we intended to make the best of my birthday weekend.

Excited to leave, my friends and I got dressed, ate breakfast, and packed at record speed. We even rushed my parents to hurry up.

Just as the clock read four o'clock, we were finally gearing up to hit the highway.

"Are y'all ready to go?" my stepdad asked us.

"Yes," we all said in sync.

"We're ready to go," I said.

"Y'all go ahead and load up in the car; here we come," my stepdad responded.

My two friends and I climbed into the back seat of my stepdad's silver Cadillac, with me sitting in the middle of them. This car meant so much to me because this was the car my stepdad taught me how to drive in, the car he let me drive to school. I also loved the color. My eyes sparkled each time I saw it, especially when it was freshly washed.

"We're about to have so much fun," Tonya said to us excitedly.

"I know; I can't wait to get there and see my cousins. I hope my cousin's friend Kenny is there. I've had a crush on him since forever," I gushed. "I know I am probably too young, and he might not look my way, but I would love to see his sexy self." I said in my flirty schoolgirl voice.

We all started laughing but quieted down when my parents walked up to the car.

"What y'all up to?" my mom asked, raising a brow.

"Nothing," we all replied with a giggle.

Once we buckled up in our seatbelts, we set off and hit the road.

♥

Cruising down the highway, my friends and I sat in the backseat talking about people at school and what we wanted to do once we made it to Indiana. I could hear my parents chatting in the front seat, but we paid very little attention to them.

As I gazed out the window, I noticed many cars on the road with us. I also saw countless corn fields, animals, and houses sitting in the middle of the country. I thought to myself, *I could do that. I could move out here in the middle of nowhere and be fine with it, away from everything and everyone.*

The sound of Mystikal's "I Smell Smoke" blared through the speakers, pulling me out of my thoughts. Tonya rapped the lyrics of the song like she had written them herself.

"What do you know about that song, Tonya?" My stepdad laughed. "You be smoking?" he asked jokingly.

"No, I just like the song," Tonya replied, laughing.

The whole car exploded with laughter. We were all laughing and joking about the song. Despite our many issues in the past, it seemed as if we were a real family, for once.

It seemed like the car ride went by quickly because we were all having fun, but it actually took four hours to get to our destination. When I spotted the root beer stand sitting at the corner when we entered Kokomo, Indiana, I knew we had made it. I could always tell just by seeing that landmark.

"Yes, we are finally here," I said out loud.

As we drove down Morgan Street and turned right onto Purdum Street, I began feeling knots in my stomach. I did not tell anyone, but I was nervous because I had told my cousin to invite his friend Kenny over to the house. Though I was expecting to see him there, I was nervous as heck because I did not know if he would like me.

After we pulled up to the house, my mind flashed back to my childhood as we all climbed out of the car. So many wonderful memories had happened on that street, in that house. I always loved it when we came to Purdum Street because that house was filled with so much love, laughter, and positivity.

I could hear "Cause I Love You" by Lenny Williams playing in the background as we walked onto the screened-in porch. My mom opened the door and walked in, and we all followed behind her. We spotted Aunt Shirley sitting on the couch with a beer in her hand. She wore her purple and gold tribal print MooMoo, her oversized nightgown, and I could tell she had been cooking because the aroma of soul food flooded the house.

My aunt smiled so big when she saw us walk through the door. She stood up excitedly, holding a

Budweiser in one hand and a Newport in the other. She greeted us all with hugs and kisses.

"I'm glad you all made it safe. How was the drive?" Aunt Shirley asked.

"It was a nice drive," my stepdad said.

"Where is Uncle Chip?" my mom asked Aunt Shirley.

"You know your uncle is at work. Where he always is, but he will be off soon," she replied.

My friends and I were all sitting around in the living room on the couch, listening to the grownups talk, when the door opened and my cousins Jimmy and Karlos walked into the house. I jumped up and ran over to them and gave both of them a hug. I introduced my two friends to them and told them they could not wait to meet them. My cousins said hello and walked over to my parents to hug them.

"Where is Kenny?" I asked my cousin Jimmy, looking toward the door.

"He just dropped us off," he replied.

"Well, call him and ask him to come back over," I said, nudging him.

Jimmy pulled out his phone and said something before hanging up. I could not hear what he said because the sweet sounds of Betty Wright's voice filled my ears.

"What did he say?" I asked once he put the phone down.

"He said he will be back over," Jimmy replied.

As soon as the words left my cousin's lips, I started smiling from ear to ear. I was now more excited, and nervous, than ever.

We heard a knock on the door as we were sitting on the floor around the coffee table, talking about what we were going to do while we were in town. Being that it was about fifteen minutes after my cousin had gotten off the phone with Kenny, I knew it was him. I could also see his face through the glass on the door. My stomach instantly started churning, but it was a good sign.

My cousin Jimmy got up and opened the door. I stared at the door, waiting to see who would walk in and, of course, it was Kenny. He was not alone, though; he had another guy with him. They walked in and spoke to everyone, and then they strolled to the back toward the kitchen.

"Cuz, come here," Jimmy said as he peeped around the wall.

I got up and walked toward the kitchen. I walked in, trying to act as normal as possible, but I prayed they could not hear my stomach.

"Keke, this is Kenny. Kenny, this is my little cousin, Keke," Jimmy said as he introduced us.

"Hello," Kenny said.

He was standing there with one hand in his pocket and the other hand holding a cell phone.

"Hello," I replied.

I sat on the floor facing the front door, looking as if I had just seen a ghost. I could not believe he was actually there and talking to me.

"So, it's your birthday, I hear."

"It's my birthday weekend. My actual birthday is tomorrow, though."

"So what are your plans?"

"I don't know. I don't have anything planned, but I want it to be a fun weekend."

"Well, we gone have to make sure it is," he smirked. "We about to go to White Castle if you and your friends want to go with us."

"Yeah, we will *all* go," Jimmy interjected. He laughed, but I knew he was serious. He had always been overprotective of me.

Even though I knew it was not a date, and Kenny was just being friendly, I thought of it as our first date. With a slight grin on my face, I walked into the living room where my parents and aunt were sitting, wondering if they would let me go to White Castle with the guys.

"What?" my mom asked as soon as she saw me. She knew I was about to ask for something.

"Jimmy and his friends are about to go to White Castle. Can we go with them, please?"

She looked me up and down. "I guess so, but don't y'all be out too late."

Before she could change her mind, I shot around the corner and told the guys we would join them. I peeped back around the corner to see if at least one of my friends was looking in my direction. When I noticed Tonya looking, I waved her over to where I stood.

"We're going to go to White Castle with the guys tonight. Y'all want to go?" I asked my friends.

"Sure, let's go." Tonya said.

We all walked out of the house and piled into two cars. Jimmy, Karlos, Tonya, Bee, and I were in one car, while Kenny and his friend were in the other one. We pulled off with Kenny's car leading the way.

Five minutes later, we pulled into the White Castle parking lot. The guys climbed out of the cars but left the car doors open with the music blasting out of the speakers. I looked out the window and noticed all the guys standing outside of the cars, rapping to the music.

I sat in the backseat for a few moments, just gazing out the window and staring at Kenny, admiring what I saw. Kenny was a short, slim guy. His chocolate skin was so silky and smooth. He had gorgeous, thick, black hair and a smile to die for. In my young eyes, I thought he was the most beautiful guy I had ever seen. I could not believe I was sitting only five feet away from my crush, and on an unofficial date with him. I was in heaven.

"Come on; let's get out," I told Tonya and Bee.

We got out and stood against the car, observing the guys interacting with each other. We watched from the sidelines while they continued rapping and talking amongst themselves.

"Girl, yo' cousin is fine as hell," Tonya blabbed to me.

"Which one?" I asked her.

"Kar-los," she said, emphasizing his name. "Keren, he is fine. I like him."

"Well, go talk to him."

As I was talking to Tonya, I noticed Bee walking toward Kenny's car and climbing into the driver's seat where Kenny's friend sat. I looked at her, wondering what she was up to. She did not know him, so I was a little confused about what she was doing and why. But I was too wrapped up in gazing at Kenny to worry about her.

"You want to go in and get something to eat," Kenny asked.

I looked around like someone was standing behind me. Then I turned back around and pointed to myself.

"Are you talking to me?" I asked him.

He smiled. "Yes, you. You want to go in and get some food?" he asked again.

"Sure, I would like that."

Kenny walked over and grabbed my hand. "Come on," he said.

I could not believe I was holding my crush's hand. My hand was probably sweating like crazy, but I definitely was not about to let his hand go, not until he let go first.

We grabbed our food and sat down at a table next to the front window. We were sitting alone, enjoying our Double Cheese Slider combos, until my cousin Jimmy came over and sat down.

"So, what are your plans for tomorrow?" Kenny asked, shifting his gaze from Jimmy to me.

"Oh, I don't have any plans," I said.

"Well, we can all go bowling or go to the movies if you want to. It's your day, so whatever you want to do."

"Okay, we can actually do both," I suggested. My body tingled with excitement at the thought of spending extra time with Kenny.

When we finished our food, we all headed back to P Block, the nickname for Purdum Street, to my cousin's house where we were staying for the weekend. Once we pulled up to the house, I got out of the car, and Kenny walked me to the door.

"I will see you tomorrow, okay?" he smiled, showing off his pearly white teeth. His eyes were so beautiful that I got lost in them as he spoke.

"Okay, I can't wait," I responded, snapping myself back into the present moment.

We parted ways, and I went into the house with my friends, leaving my cousins outside with theirs. Exhausted from all the traveling and excitement, I was ready to lie down and get the next day started. I felt like a little kid on Christmas Eve awaiting Christmas morning. All cozy in my pajamas with a grin on my face, I drifted off to sleep with thoughts of Kenny running through my mind.

♥

I woke up knowing it had to be the next morning because I smelled breakfast cooking and the sound of Millie Jackson blasting through the house. My stomach growled as the smell of fresh onions, fried potatoes, bacon, and biscuits tickled my nose.

Yes, Aunt Shirley is cooking, I thought to myself.

Eager to start my day, I sat up in the bed and glanced over at my friends; they were still asleep. I wiped the sleep from my eyes, inhaling the aroma of Aunt Shirley's wrist work. I walked into the kitchen and noticed my mom, my stepdad, and Uncle Chip sitting at the kitchen table. Aunt Shirley stood over the stove finishing up breakfast.

I walked over and planted a kiss on my aunt's cheek and topped it off with a side hug. Next, I said good morning to Uncle Chip and gave him a hug and kiss, too.

"Sit down and have some breakfast, chile," my aunt told me. "Your friends still sleep?"

"Yes, they were tired when we got in last night," I replied.

"So, what are you all going to get into today?" my mom asked with her left eyebrow high in the air, clearly trying to dig for some information.

"Well, Jimmy and his friends are going to take us bowling and to the movies tonight," I said with a smile on my face as wide as the Grinch's.

My mom said nothing but continued giving me the side eye as Aunt Shirley fixed our plates.

I sat at the table with my family, trying to be present in the moment, but all I could think about was what the night had in store. Would we really be going bowling and to the movies? Would Kenny cancel because of other plans? I mean, it was Valentine's Day, so he could have had a girlfriend and something planned with her. So many thoughts and emotions stirred on the inside of me. Imagining how I would feel if Kenny stood me up bothered me the most.

After damn near thinking myself into a panic attack, the evening finally had arrived. Family members had come over to my aunt's house earlier, like they did on most days. You could hear the music pumping, people laughing and talking, and everyone enjoying themselves. Now that a good day of hanging out with my family and friends had ended, it was time to get ready for my night with Kenny.

My cousin Jimmy walked into the sitting room with his keys in hand. In a booming voice, he asked, "Are you ready?"

"Yes, we are." Butterflies fluttered in my stomach as I thought about my follow-up question. "Are Kenny 'nem here yet?"

"No, they are going to meet us there, but since we waited so late, we are just going to go to the movies instead of bowling."

"Okay," I said with a little hesitation. Though I was disappointed, I figured I could still have some alone time with Kenny.

My friends and I climbed into the car with my two cousins, ready to see what the night had to offer. It was officially my night, and I was definitely going to make the best of it.

"What took you all so long?" Kenny asked Jimmy when we pulled up to the movie theater.

"They took forever getting dressed," Jimmy responded, looking back at me and my friends.

I glanced down at my blue jean hip huggers, white dress shirt, and blue and white vest. I had to look extra good for Kenny, so it was worth the wait.

Kenny stood outside his car in the parking lot, sporting some black jeans and a black hoodie, along with long black braids. I sat in the car admiring him, thinking about how good he looked in all black.

After many days and nights of dreaming about going out with Kenny, I was finally getting my shot. I felt like I was Dorothy from *The Wizard of Oz* clicking my heels, saying there's no place like home.

"Why you looking like that?"

I turned toward Tonya's voice. She looked at me and smirked. "You scared?"

"I don't know. I'm excited, but I'm nervous as hell." I scanned the parking lot and then leaned in closer to my friends. "I'm so nervous that I have the bubble guts."

"Well, it's too late for that now," Bee said. "Get your butt out and go say 'hi' to that fine boy."

I nodded and then swallowed the air in my throat.

As we exited the car and headed toward the circle with the guys, my cousin told us to come on because the movie was about to start.

When Kenny grabbed my hand, my stomach dropped. My heart started pounding so fast that I became even more anxious. Cool and collected, Kenny led me inside the movie theater doors and right up to the cashier's counter.

"Two tickets for *Fallen*," Kenny told Becky, the cashier. Her name, printed in big letters, covered the badge on her shirt.

"Sure, fourteen dollars, please," Becky replied.

Kenny eased into his pocket with no hesitation. He pulled out the money and handed it to the cashier. The cashier took the money and handed Kenny two tickets.

"You will be in theater three," Becky informed us with a warm smile.

Kenny turned in my direction. "You want some popcorn?"

"Sure," I told him.

We walked side by side to the concession counter, and it seemed like I was gliding on a big, fluffy cloud. My cheeks hurt from the huge smile plastered on my face. The feeling mirrored those exaggerated displays of joy from the corny movies I had seen on TV. I thought to myself, *Girl, pinch his ass because this definitely can't be real*. I let off a slight chuckle to myself, thankful Kenny could not read my mind.

His voice interrupted my thoughts seconds later. "What you want to eat on?"

"I will take a medium popcorn with extra butter and a small Dr. Pepper," I told the tall, lanky guy waiting behind the counter.

Again, Kenny went into his pockets and paid the cashier. The guy handed me my food and drink, and then Kenny and I walked to theater three.

Kenny stepped in front of me and opened the door for me. I stopped as soon as I crossed the threshold, waiting to see where Kenny wanted to sit. We looked around, and I could see the rest of the group sitting halfway down the theater on the left side.

Kenny turned around and looked at me. "Come on."

He led me down the aisle, and I followed him, thinking we were going to sit with the rest of the group. Instead of walking to the left toward the group, he shifted to the right, where we would be the only two in that row and away from our friends.

As soon as we sat down, the lights went out. I stuck my hands in my popcorn, and I felt Kenny's arm around my shoulders. I turned and looked at him and then flashed my schoolgirl smile.

I sat in Kenny's arms for an hour and a half, the length of the entire movie. It did not matter if I went right back to the house after the movie; I was already satisfied with my night.

"So, what's next on the agenda?" my cousin Jimmy asked.

"Well, let's go and find something to eat," Kenny's friend Dallas replied.

"Are you going to ride with me?" Kenny asked as he grabbed my hand.

"Yes, sure," I blushed.

I got in the car with Kenny and his friend Dallas, and my friends got in the car with my two cousins. Dallas sat in the backseat, and I slid into the front seat next to Kenny.

"We're going to follow, y'all," Kenny yelled out the window to my cousin.

Jimmy's car pulled off, and Kenny put the car in gear and pulled off behind my cousin. As I sat there inhaling the smell of Kenny's cologne and listening to Tupac's "All Eyez on Me" booming through the speakers, I wondered if this was how it would be if I were there with him, if I were his girl.

I looked out the front windshield and spotted my cousin's car going through a red light. Seconds later, Kenny got stuck at the light. I thought my cousin would have pulled over and waited for us, but he kept going. When the light turned green, my cousins and my friends were nowhere in sight.

"Damn, where did they go?" Kenny asked, interrupting the silence.

We rode through the streets, hitting the main hangouts and the main streets to see if they were around the area, but each place we searched showed no traces of Jimmy or his car. Kenny tried calling Jimmy, but his phone repeatedly went straight to voicemail.

After driving around for about an hour and a half, we pulled up to a big, beautiful house. I glanced out the car window, wondering where we were, yet deciding not to ask any questions.

"You want to go in my house for a second? Maybe they will pop up here?" Kenny asked, his eyes glistening in the darkness.

Though I replied, "sure", I was a little concerned because I had not been around Kenny much and I was alone without my cousins or my friends. Being violated as a young child made me skeptical of certain situations, this one included. Good things hardly ever happened when I was left alone.

We hopped out of the car, and Kenny called out to his friend in the backseat to wake him up. Kenny must have sensed I was a little nervous because he grabbed my hand.

"It's okay. We're just going to watch a little TV for a little bit."

"I'm okay," I told him, though my heartbeat told another story.

We entered the house, and Kenny led me to the living room and escorted me to the couch, inviting me to have a seat. His friend sat in a chair positioned counterclockwise from the couch. Kenny grabbed the remote control and turned on the TV and then sat next to me on the couch.

I sat there with my head facing the TV while stealing glimpses of him from the corner of my eye. I was elated to be in his presence yet nervous because it was already getting late and I was not trying to piss my parents off. But when I focused back on the moment, I was willing to take the punishment. He was worth it.

After flicking through the channels for a few minutes, Kenny stopped on the hit sitcom *Martin*. It was the episode where Martin accused Gina and his friends of stealing his Walkman CD player. They were all dressed in black sitting at the table as Martin walked around with the stuffed rottweiler dog. The episode was hilarious, and I remembered the exact scene he was acting out from the movie *New Jack City*. I started laughing hysterically, but my laughter died down once Kenny's phone rang.

Being the insecure girl I was, jealousy consumed my mind. I wondered, *Who the heck is calling his phone this late at night? What girl wants to talk to him? What girl does he talk to because I'm not in the same city as him and he must have someone who is keeping him occupied?* My mind was getting the best of me, but the intrusive thoughts ceased once he hung up the phone.

"That was Jimmy. They at the house. I can take you there if you are ready," Kenny said.

Look at my paranoid ass thinking it was a girl, and the whole time it was my cousin. I laughed inside.

"Yeah, I probably should head that way because I don't want my parents to trip."

Kenny turned off the TV and told his friend to come on. We left the house and headed for my cousin's house. Because it was not far, it did not take us long to arrive.

As soon as the car stopped, I opened the door and got out. Kenny followed me. He grabbed my hand and walked me to the outside door of my aunt and uncle's house, which led to their closed-in porch.

When we stopped in front of the door, Kenny gave me his number. "Make sure you call me."

"I will." I glanced at the ground and then back up at him. "Thank you for spending my birthday with me. I appreciate it."

"It was no problem at all. I didn't know you liked me, and I had a good time. This won't be the last time." He smiled.

Kenny grabbed me by the waist and pulled me closer to him. I wrapped my arms around him, and then he kissed me on my lips. I felt my stomach knotting up from the butterflies fluttering in it.

He went in for another kiss, but this time he separated my lips with his tongue. I felt his tongue going in and out of my mouth, and I mirrored his actions, wondering if I was doing it right.

As Kenny kissed me, I felt a throbbing between my legs, and I knew it was time for me to get my butt in the house. I gave him another peck on the lips and told him I would call him once I made it back home. I thanked him again before disappearing into the house.

I tiptoed through the living room, trying to be as quiet as a mouse. Then I grabbed some cover and lay down on the couch. I thought I was in the clear until I heard my cousin Jimmy's voice.

"So where did y'all go?" he asked.

"Y'all went through the light and left us. We didn't know where y'all went, so he rode around, then we went back to his house and watched *Martin* until you called."

"Mmm hmm," he said, raising a brow.

"For real," I chuckled. A few seconds later, I rolled over and went to sleep with Kenny and that kiss on my mind.

The next morning was bittersweet. It was Sunday morning, and our trip had come to an end. It was time to head back to Illinois. This time, I was sad not because I was going back home to my abuser, but because I was going to be 200 miles away from the boy whom I had just grown closer to, whom I was sure I loved.

Chapter 8

Even though I entertained other guys, I remained in contact with Kenny as my freshman year continued. He and my cousins even came to see me once. I could not control my excitement because I missed him so much, and because I had something else on my mind.

In the weeks leading up to their visit, I reminisced about the time I spent with Kenny in Indiana and fantasized about all the things we could do together. Just from our phone conversations, I could see us doing way more than kissing and hugging. I could see us going all the way.

When Kenny finally made it to my city, it was such a special visit because that weekend was the weekend I lost my virginity on my own, not from being forced. I could not have planned it more perfectly myself.

My cousins went out to sightsee, leaving me and Kenny in the hotel room alone. Before I knew it, we were acting out the things I had envisioned in my mind, kissing, touching, rubbing. Everything! I had wanted this to happen for a while, and I was more than ready for it. I just wish that feeling could have lasted forever.

♥

Like the other teenagers at my school, I busied myself with the high school stunt shows and the homecoming dance to distract myself from the boys. Before the homecoming dance, the school held a program called "The Stunt Shows". The Stunt Shows usually occurred a couple of days before the dance. Every class presented its own skits one after another and all on the same day. Though I did not have a date for the dance, a couple of my friends and I decided to attend as a group.

As usual, my cousin Shauna kept my hair done every weekend, so I did not have to worry about my hair for the dance. Shauna also agreed to help me search for a homecoming outfit. While I did not care for large crowds, I was excited to go to the homecoming dance because it would be my first one.

I wonder who all is going to be there, I thought as I got dressed for The Stunt Shows event. I was excited yet nervous because I did not know what to expect.

"Who is it?" I heard my grandmother ask after hearing someone knock on the front door.

I hurried to the door, trying to slide past her, but it was too late. My grandma had just embarrassed the shit out of me; she had opened the front door butt-ass naked.

Frozen in place, I stood there with my eyes bucked and my mouth wide open. I stared at my grandma in disbelief. I looked out the door and spotted my friends standing on the porch with their mouths gaped open as well. As soon as my grandma hit the corner to walk back toward her bedroom, they burst out gagging.

"Did she really just open that door naked?" one of my friends said, laughing.

"Omg, I'm so sorry, y'all. Please excuse my grandma and her saggy booty," I said, heat spreading across my face from the embarrassment. "Give me a second to get my things. I will be right back and then we can go."

Despite my grandmother's peep show, my friends and I had a good time at The Stunt Shows with our classmates and the other students. It was so much fun, and I already could not wait for the next year's stunt shows. Thankfully, no one brought up the incident with my grandmother that night. We were able to keep our thoughts off of her naked body and on the amazing stunt shows that had just taken place.

We did not know it then, but things were about to get more interesting as we left the school. I jumped into the car with my friends, including Tracy and her older sister, Tiffany, and we headed to Big Street because Tiffany had left her jacket at some dude's house. Though the night was clear, the air was a little mild and reeking of stale smoke. As we sat in the car waiting for Tiffany to walk back outside, a car pulled up behind us with its lights off.

"Who is that?" Tracy asked.

I turned to look out the back window. "I'm not sure. I can't see anyone."

The doors opened, and someone got out of the car and started walking toward us.

"What are you girls doing over here?" a police officer spoke through the passenger side window.

The officer stood there looking directly into the car, eyeing each of us with a notepad and pen in his hand.

"We came over here to get my sister's jacket," Tracy replied to the officer.

The officer stood there, straight and tall, with an annoyed look on his face. He asked yet another question. "Where are you girls coming from?"

"From the stunt shows," we all said in unison.

"We had reports of shots being fired," the officer informed us.

While I hoped everyone was okay, I wondered why he would come to *our* car, a car full of girls. *What could we have possibly done?* I thought.

At that point, Tiffany emerged from the house. The officer took his attention off us and focused on her instead. We were all sitting in the car with confused looks on our faces, still clueless about what was going on, and a little terrified, too.

"I need you girls to come down to the police station for some questioning," the police officer said.

Though he seemed pretty nice, you could not tell from his stern face and authoritative voice. His facial expression said he did not completely believe us, but we were telling the truth.

As we drove to the police station, I could not shake the thought of whether we would be arrested. Even though we had no clue about what had happened on that street before we got there, that had not stopped police from locking people up in the past just to have an arrest.

Officer "Stern Face" led us to an extremely cold and bright white room after we arrived at the police station. Only a long rectangular table and about six brown chairs occupied the room.

"Have a seat," the officer instructed us.

We all grabbed a chair and nervously sat down in front of the officer.

"So, let's try this again," the officer said, with a little more authority this time, probably because we were on his stomping grounds now.

"Now, what were you girls doing on that street, at that house, and at this time of night?" the officer asked us.

"We were just leaving The Stunt Shows at Central and stopped by there on our way home because I had left my jacket over there earlier today," Tiffany responded.

The officer watched Tiffany closely and then continued his questioning. "So you girls don't know anything about the shooting that took place over there today?"

"Look, I told you we were just leaving the homecoming stunt shows and we have no clue about a shooting," Tiffany responded again, clearly frustrated.

"I'm trying to help you girls out, but I need you to be honest with me about why you were parked in front of that house, and I need to know about that shooting," the officer retorted as he mirrored Tiffany's frustration.

With a roll of her eyes, Tiffany said, "I don't know how many times I have to say it, but we can't tell you about anything we don't know anything about, and if you are not arresting us, I believe we are free to go, right?"

The officer stared at Tiffany for a moment before responding. "Yes, you are free to go, but let me give you girls some advice. Those guys are not good guys, and you should really be careful about where you hang and who you call a friend."

"We will," we all said in sync. Then we hopped up from the table and sprinted out of the police station.

The ride home was extremely quiet. I was sure everyone was lost in their thoughts because I definitely was. I sat there thanking God that we were let go and I could make it home without my grandma finding out where I was.

I still bunked with my grandmother because she lived in the Central District and my parents had moved, meaning I would have had to attend another school. I wanted to stay where I was, so living with my grandmother was the only option. After that run-in with the police, I had never been so ready to go home in my life. I do not know how my grandmother found out about the incident, but she did.

The weekend had passed, and I was sitting on the couch watching *Sister Sister*. It was the episode where Tia and Tamera were in the school talent show. They were Roger's background singers as he sang "Do You Love Me" by The Contours.

As I sat there enjoying the episode, I heard footsteps creeping up behind me and knew it was my grandma sauntering into the living room. I turned around to look at her, and she was standing there in her bath towel, a *National Enquire* in one hand and a can of old-style beer in the other hand, with no wig on her head. I looked at her and just shook my head.

"So you wasn't going to tell me that you were down at the police station the other night for questioning about a shooting?" she asked, taking a sip of her beer.

I gulped. "I didn't tell you because I didn't think it was important being that we were in no trouble and we didn't know anything."

"Yo' ass go to the police station for questioning, but yo' dumb ass don't think it's important enough to tell me? I buy your dumb ass books and send you to school, and your ass still don't learn," she fussed.

I sat there quietly and let her talk. Though I heard her words, they entered one ear and went right back out the other one.

Anyone who knew my grandmother knew she would cuss you out in 2.5 seconds. She did not care who you were or where she was. As her family, we all learned how to ignore her fussing, insults, and cussing. If she was not cussing anyone out, that was the time to worry because she might have been sick.

"I know your big forehead ass hear me talking to you," she said, noticing my attention had drifted elsewhere.

"Grandma, I heard you. What do you want me to say? I'm sorry." The irritation and attitude in my voice spoke volumes.

"I should knock yo' ass out," she said, glaring at me. She definitely had gotten the message.

I looked up at her with the "I wish you would" look, but I knew damn well if she did hit me, I would not do anything to her. But in my mind, I had pushed her little shit-talking ass down.

"Since you want to sit there and just look retarded, you can go back to your momma and daddy's house and get on their nerves," she spat.

I rolled my eyes on the low, just enough to feel it but not enough for her to see it, and responded with a simple "okay".

By the weekend, I was packing my clothes and moving back home with my parents. I think my grandmother thought she was hurting me, but she wasn't because things at home had become better, much better than they had been in the past. The only downside was, instead of walking a block up the street to get to school, I now had to walk about a mile.

♥

Every day, a group of us kids, about eight of us, would walk home together because we all lived on the same route. On the walk home, I noticed this senior from the school who would drive by us. Each time I saw his car roll by, I would get so excited. The biggest smile would spread across my face, and I would grab one of my friends by the arm and tell her, “Look, girl, there he is.”

The only thing I knew about this mystery guy was that he was fine as hell and he drove a maroon Chrysler Dynasty. I also knew when it was time for him to cruise down the street. Each time he drove by, I would get butterflies, and I could feel them fluttering all over. I had not had a crush like that since Kenny, my first.

I knew I wanted to be this guy’s girlfriend, but I figured he wouldn’t want me because I was an underclassman and he was a senior. I was not going to lose hope, though. As I waited for my crush to notice me, I entertained a couple of other seniors from the school.

One of the seniors worked at Taco Bell; he was so fine and clean-cut. He definitely noticed me and flirted with me all the time. We eventually exchanged numbers and talked on the phone. However, Mr. Taco Bell and Mr. Chrysler did not get along, not because of me, but for their own personal reasons. Even though I did not know about their beef in the beginning, I found out about it when they fought. I know I should not have been talking to both of them, but I figured why not. I was not in a relationship with anyone, and I was fresh in high school. So I thought, *Bring on the boys.*

Of course, they all had government names, but I gave them nicknames. This was the secret code my sister

Brandi and I shared. All I had to do was mention a nickname, and she would know exactly who I was talking about.

Then it finally happened. I found myself skipping around the house one day because I had some great news to tell Brandi. Butterflies filled my stomach, my heart raced, and a huge smile covered my face. Once my nerves settled, I picked up the house phone and dialed my sister's number.

"Hello?"

"What you doing?" I asked with a smile, excited to hear my sister's voice on the other end of the receiver.

"Nothing, was sitting here watching TV."

"Girl, guess what?" I squealed.

"What?" she asked, thirsty for the gossip.

"So, I asked Chrysler if he would go to homecoming with me, and he said yeah," I gushed.

"Hold on, so how did y'all even begin to talk because last time I checked, he was still a crush?"

After letting out a sigh, I gave her nosey butt all the details. "Well, I was walking home from school, and he rode by me. I kept walking, but when I reached Burger King, he was sitting in the parking lot. I got close to his car, and he said, 'Aye, can you come here for a second?' I walked over there, and he said he had been checking me out and wanted to know if he could have my number. So, of course, I gave it to him . . . we've been talking on the phone for about a week now."

"So, how you get away with that? You know your stepdaddy not having that," she laughed.

She knew my stepdad was extremely overprotective when it came to boys. The only boy he approved of me talking to on the phone, or even going out with, was a guy we coded as "Church Boy".

"Most times he has his sister ask for me. When I get on the phone, she passes the phone over to him." I paused as my dilemma rushed to the forefront of my mind. "I have two weeks to come up with an outfit and a plan to convince my parents to let me go to homecoming with him."

"Okay, well answer this question, sister girl. What you going to do about Lips?"

"Shit," I said, forgetting all about me talking to Lips.

Lips was a dark, smooth-skinned brother with big lips. He stood at medium height and was slightly thin but cut up; he had nice muscles. When I looked at Lips, I thought about the character Caine from the movie *Menace II Society*. Just fine. Too fine.

I had been so consumed with Chrysler that I had not thought about what I was going to do about Lips. It should not have been too difficult of a task, though. Lips was not allowed on school property because he had been expelled. Besides, we were not in a relationship, so why did I have to suffer?

♥

Not long after the homecoming dance, I was walking down Thrush Street one day on my way to grab some snacks from the gas station. I rocked some blue jeans, a red sweatshirt, and white gym shoes. My hair was pulled back in a long ponytail.

As I hit the corner, a little gray station wagon pulled up beside me. I looked at the car and was somewhat shocked, thinking, *What is this handsome guy doing driving this little bug?* I laughed to myself and shook my head, hoping to shake away my petty thoughts.

"Hey, cutie! What's your name?" he called out to me.

I stood there, still lost in my thoughts, but somehow, I managed to say, "Keren."

"You stay around here? Can I give you a ride?" he asked.

"No, I don't know you, and I'm only going to the gas station." I smiled to hide my annoyance.

"Well, Keren, may I get your number to maybe call you sometime?"

"My stepdad really doesn't allow me to have boys call the house, but I will take yours."

I was still standing outside of the car, but I could see him looking around for a pen and some paper to write his number on.

"Here you go. Now don't take this number if you not going to use it, cutie," he teased.

"I wouldn't take it if I wasn't," I responded with my hand on my hip and a little sass in my voice.

"Well, you have a good day, cutie," he said.

"Thank you, and you do the same."

I instantly felt a knot in my stomach during that first interaction. Something about him just did not sit right with me. I could not put my hand on it then, but being that I was young and naive, I just ignored it.

Chapter 9

Remember the guy who asked me for my number at the gas station? His name was Chucky Jr., and his code name was Clown Car. Even though I was feeling him, I still communicated with my other guy friends. I had to keep my options open, as usual.

From the outside looking in, you would have thought Chucky Jr. and I had a pretty good relationship, as far as young relationships go. Don't get me wrong: it was good in the beginning. Chucky Jr. would tell me everything I wanted and needed to hear. He was charming, attentive, caring, generous, protective, and supportive. Well, at least that is what he led me to believe.

This guy had me so open and into him that I started sneaking out of the house and stealing my mom's car, her white Chevrolet Beretta, just to visit him, even if only for a few minutes. While I do not know why, I just had to be near him.

I thought everything was perfect until about six months after we met. That's when Chucky Jr. came over to my house and revealed his little secret.

The sun was still poking through the clouds as the evening approached. We had the front door open, allowing some fresh air to flow through the screen door. I was sitting in the living room watching *Family Matters* when I heard someone tapping on the screen door.

"Hey, what's going on?" I said to Chucky Jr. as I walked out to the porch.

"Not too much, just came outside for a minute. Been in the house all day." He looked down. "I wasn't feeling too good. I was itching on my stomach going down toward my private area. I pulled my shirt up and let my mom see, and she said that I have crabs."

I instantly gave him the "who-pooted" face.

"You have what?" I asked him through gritted teeth.

"I believe I have crabs. I went to CVS to get some stuff to clear it up, and I think you should, too."

My face grew hot. "Who the hell you been screwing to give yo' stupid ass crabs?" I yelled.

"I haven't been with anyone. I was going to ask you who you were with because I know for a fact that I haven't been sleeping with no one else."

For a split second, I almost believed him. I knew I had not been sleeping around with anyone, and I knew he did not catch the shit from me. But little ol' dumb me. I continued to deal with his lying, cheating ass. I thought he would have realized he had made a mistake and gotten his shit together, but that was just the beginning of a long downward spiral between the two of us.

Within two years, Chucky and I went from visiting each other every day to seeing each other all day, every day. I moved out of my mom's house during my junior year of high school and moved in with this man, who I thought loved me. Almost overnight, the nice guy act went sour, and the real Chucky rose to the surface.

Our place was a small, one-bedroom apartment in a brick building. Four apartments occupied the complex, which was near my aunt's house. Even though we were technically neighbors, I did not get to see my aunt much, or anyone else for that matter.

I attended school during the day and worked at St. Francis Hospital in the cafeteria as a cashier in the evening. The position did not offer many hours, but I enjoyed it because I could get away from Chucky Jr. and have conversations with people other than him and his family and friends. The only person I connected with in Chucky's family was Sabrina, his cousin on his mother's side of the family.

Chucky had become so possessive of me that it was not cute anymore. I used to think it was sweet. Hell, I even thought it meant he loved me, but there was nothing sweet about me having to be around only him, his friends, and his family. I did not know it then, but he was insecure and maybe even guilty because his ass was doing foul shit behind my back.

A little over a year had passed since Chucky Jr. and I moved in together, and I sat at the dining room table one night thinking about how unhappy I was. Chucky sat on the couch watching *In Living Color*. His obnoxious laughing drowned out my thoughts.

After the crabs incident, I slowly began reconnecting with my guy friends. Chucky Jr. would drop me off at school, and I would leave school shortly after. I would go to Lips's house until school was near dismissal and then get dropped right back off at school so that Chucky could pick me up.

All Lips and I would do was roll up and smoke and watch a TV show or a movie. I would have my friend, Amy, write a note almost every day, saying I had to go to the doctor or some other lie to excuse me from my 5th-period and 6th-period classes. I just needed some exhale time, and I was about to get a little more of it.

One afternoon around 2:45 p.m., I sat outside of the high school on the stairs, talking to a couple of friends while waiting for Chucky to pick me up. No more Mr. Clown Car, he pulled up in his red convertible car. When I spotted him, I slowly rose from my seat. Then I sighed and told my friends bye.

"How was your day?" Chucky asked as we pulled off.

"It was good. How was court?" I could tell something was occupying his mind. I knew he was worried because he had to appear before a judge for repeatedly driving with no license.

"It was okay." He paused. "The judge said I have to do a month and some days in the county."

I could hear the worry in his voice, and I could see it in his eyes.

"What? Wow. Why?" I stuttered. I was almost speechless.

"He said my fine wasn't paid in time. I have to turn myself in within a week, and there is no way out of it."

Though initially upset because I would have to be alone, I was lowkey excited because I knew I would have some peace for at least a month. I could relax and visit with family and friends I had not seen in a while. I could attend some events I had been wanting to attend. After being under Chucky's thumb for so long, I planned to use this time alone to get in the streets and to get some well-needed relaxation.

"Damn, I'm sorry." I paused. "It's only a month, though, and I'm not going anywhere, so I'll be here." I said, being a supportive girlfriend.

And guess what I got in return? Not one thank you. Not one I love you. Nothing. He shot me a stank look and rolled his eyes. I could not believe this negro had the nerve to roll his big ass eyes at me when I was trying to be there to support him. That gesture alone kicked my "fuck you" attitude into full gear.

The next week could not come fast enough. When the day finally arrived for Chucky to turn himself in, I was ready to roll his ass down Maxwell Road without stopping.

"Well, here I go. Take care of my car. Love ya," he said, as he exited the car.

"I love you, too," I responded. I honestly did, but I was excited to get a break from him.

Once he was out of view, I drove off into the sunset. Not exactly, but that is how I felt at that moment. I felt like the queen of the world.

As soon as I left the county jail, I drove straight to Garfield Street—where my mom's baby brother and my favorite uncle, Skeeter, and his wife, Maggie, lived—to get some weed so that I could free my mind. Later, I would go bowling with one of my coworkers. She had been trying to get me to hang out with her for a while, and I was finally going to take her up on her offer.

I was as calm as a cucumber, as the effects of some good weed and Remy Martin VSOP filled my body. Once almost too afraid to let it take effect, I had come a long way since the first time I tried marijuana. I felt so mellow and unbothered, and I was feeling myself. I wore a cute blue jean one-piece outfit and some black clog heels. I had even straightened my hair out with a fresh silk press. This girl was ready to see what the night had to offer.

"Hey, girl. I'm glad you're finally able to get away," my coworker joked as she got in the car.

"Yeah, the warden let me out tonight," I replied with a chuckle.

"Well, it's a girls' night, and I'm going to make sure you enjoy it because you need it. You're too young to be so stressed out the way you do."

She was so right. I felt like I was wasting my life away. I needed to be enjoying my life instead of living a miserable one.

My coworker and I spent that night savoring some drinks and delighting in some girl talk while bowling a couple of games. When I made it back home, it was 2:30 in the morning. I did not realize I had stayed out so long, but it felt so good not to worry about checking the time or my surroundings. That day was definitely a good day.

♥

Despite my newfound freedom, I still had to fulfill my girlfriend duties. Two weeks after Chucky Jr. turned himself in, I planned a trip to visit him. His brother wanted to ride with me, so I told him he could. On the following Saturday, I scooped his brother up, and we headed to the county jail.

"I need your license and registration," the county officer barked when we arrived. They were conducting a safety check in the parking lot. The officer explained they performed random checks like that occasionally.

I handed him the information he needed and looked at my brother-in-law while he searched for his ID to give to the other officer standing on the passenger side of the car.

"Do you guys have anything illegal in this car?" the officer asked.

"No, nothing," I replied, not even considering the possibility.

First, there was silence, then out of nowhere, I heard Chucky Jr.'s brother open his mouth: "All I have is this."

I looked over, and he pulled out a beer he had sitting between his legs. The officer took his beer and told us, "I need you both to step out the car."

After we stepped out of the car, the officers escorted us to the back of the vehicle where they searched us before searching the car.

"What's this?" the officer asked as he held up an empty sandwich bag.

"I don't know, officer," I answered. "This is my boyfriend's car. I was driving it to come and visit him."

"You know I could charge you with this bag," the officer said matter-of-factly.

"But the bag is empty," I said, the confusion clear in my voice.

"It's empty, but there is white residue on this bag. I could charge you for it, but I'm going to let you guys go since we didn't find anything else. But you need to be careful who you ride in the car with, and tell your boyfriend he needs to keep his car clean."

Even though the officer did not take me to jail, he still charged me with the transportation of alcohol. We also could not attend the visit that week. I was so pissed off at Chucky Jr. because the bag with the white residue on it had to be his, not to mention I got a damn ticket because of his dumb ass brother.

I needed someone to talk to about what had happened. Because I did not want to hear the lecture my parents would give me, I called Chucky Jr.'s dad, Chucky Sr.

"Hello," Chucky Sr. said, his deep voice bellowing through the phone.

"Hi, Mr. Chucky. This is Keren, and I was wondering if I could come down to your house to talk to you about a few things," I asked him, embarrassed beyond belief.

"Of course, you can. I usually make it home from work around six. You can come by then or wait 'til the weekend," he responded.

"Okay, that's fine. I can wait 'til Saturday."

"I'll be home after three."

"I'll see you then, Mr. Chucky. Thank you and have a good day," I said as I ended the call.

I did not talk to Chucky Jr.'s family much, but he had some family members whom I loved, and some whom I cared nothing about. Chucky Sr. was one of the family members I loved. I could talk to him about anything, and he would tell me what I needed to hear, even if it was to leave his son alone, live my life, and be happy.

Trying to steel my nerves, I knocked on Chucky Sr.'s door on Saturday evening. As I stood there waiting for him to answer, I wondered what to say to him. Would my words make him mad? Would he try to take up for his son? So many thoughts rushed through my mind, but I knew I had to get them out.

"Hey, Keren; come on in," Mr. Chucky said as he opened the screen door.

I walked in nervously and followed him to the dining room table.

"You want something to drink?" he asked as he opened the cabinet and grabbed a glass.

"Yes, please," I responded courteously.

Mr. Chucky was an attractive older man. I emphasized older because he was my boyfriend's dad. He had brown-toned skin and a tall, medium build. He also wore glasses. I could tell he used to get all the women back in the day. Unfortunately, his son thought he could do the same thing.

"So, what did you want to talk to me about, Keren," he asked.

"Well, Mr. Chucky," I swallowed a gulp of air. "I don't know what to do about your son, sir. I care about him and love him, but I'm tired of him talking to me crazy. I'm tired of him putting me down. I'm tired of him being mean. I'm tired of being played like a dummy, sir." I paused to catch my breath. "I went to visit him last week, and the police had safety checks on the cars that entered the parking lot. They found a sandwich bag with white residue on it. That officer was talking about taking me to jail." My voice broke. "I don't know what to do, sir. I need your advice."

Chucky Sr. paused for a moment and then leaned forward. "Listen to me loud and clear, Keren. You are a young, smart, and beautiful girl. You have your whole life ahead of you, and you are too young to be worrying about these types of problems. The only thing you should be worried about is your grades. I don't care if it's my son or not, you don't deserve that, and life is way too short to be stressing about the bull. You need to worry about yourself and what you are going to do to be a success. Worry about what college you are going to go to and not what some boy is doing. If he don't treat you right, then do what you have to do."

Agreeing with everything he said, I nodded as the tears flowed. I soaked up all his words, making sure I was listening, and listening fully.

"Thank you, Mr. Chucky. I appreciate you taking the time out to listen to me and offer me some advice. I really needed to hear that."

"Look, I will make a deal with you. If you focus on your studies, graduate from high school, and enroll in college, I will pay your tuition," he told me with much sincerity.

I lifted my head to look him in the face, and he was staring me right in the eyes. His eyes told me he was not joking at all. He was serious.

"Really, Mr. Chucky?" My eyes lit up. "Wow! I promise you I will do exactly that. I promise!"

I did not know if he would keep his promise, but I knew he did not have any reason to lie to me. Regardless, I was going to do whatever it took to finish high school and enroll in college. I had made a promise, and I planned on keeping it.

Chapter 10

I finally made it to my senior year of high school in the fall of 2000. All I could think about was that I was almost there and there was nothing that could stand in the way of me getting my diploma. I just knew it was going to be an easy and laid-back year for me. I could see my future so clearly, and I thought constantly about what the future had in store.

With only eight months until I became a high school graduate, I knew I wanted to go to college to study criminal justice because I had always wanted to study some type of law. I wanted to live on campus, join a sorority, and travel the world before settling down and starting a family.

I also knew I did not want to continue living the life I lived with Chucky Jr. No part of me wanted to continue living with the constant arguing and unhappiness, nor did I want to go through life with any regrets.

How was I supposed to get out of this relationship that had become so toxic? I asked myself this question frequently as the end of the school year drew closer. I once asked myself this question while sitting on the couch in our apartment, finishing up some homework.

Chucky Jr.'s loud and aggressive voice broke my concentration. He must have called my name before, but I was too consumed with thoughts of my future to hear him.

"Keren, I'm not going to call your name again," Chucky growled.

"Huh, what did you say?" I asked him, confused.

"If you can 'huh', you can hear. Yo' ass hear what the hell you want to hear," he fussed.

I did not respond to him because I knew if I would have said anything, it would have continued on, and I was not in the mood to argue.

"I know you heard me. Why you acting dumb like you didn't? You get on my nerves with that dumb shit," he nagged.

"Who the fuck you talking to?" I snapped back.

Forgetting all about being quiet, I was pissed the hell off at this point. I was not the type to argue, and I was guilty of letting stuff slide, but I refused to tolerate disrespect. Somehow, I found the strength to stand up for myself.

"Oh, now you can hear me? Well, hear this: I'm going to Texas with my dad for a few days, and I am leaving tomorrow," he hissed.

"So, you tell me the day before? So convenient of you. Thanks for the heads up." The sarcasm oozed from my lips.

"I do believe I am grown. It's not like I have to ask you, and be happy I did tell you at all," he yelled.

"You right. Go ahead and do what the hell you want to do, and that's exactly what I'm going to do also. So, see ya," I yelled back as I opened the door to our apartment.

As I attempted to walk outside, I heard him trying to put some bass in his voice.

"Keren, stop playing with me! Don't make me fuck you up," he shouted. The veins popped up in his neck.

"Nigga, who is playing? I'm tired of yo' shit, so go on to Texas and have fun." I smirked.

As the words left my lips, I felt a force push me forward. The push was heavy enough to make me trip, but not hard enough to make me fall. I caught my balance and turned to face him.

"What the hell is your problem?" I shouted. "You better keep your hands off of me!"

"Or what? I told you to quit playing with me, Keren."

"You better quit playing with ya self and leave me the hell alone!"

As I listened to my own words, I instantly thought to myself, *Why in the hell do I continue to go back and forth with this idiot? Just shut up and let him go on about his business*. But my crazy ass just could not do that. I was caught up in a toxic cycle.

"I fucking hate you," I screamed.

"Hate yo' ass in that damn house," he yelled.

"You not my damn daddy. You can't tell me what to do." I stood there with my hand on my hip and my neck twirling in circles.

When Chucky Jr. pushed me this time, I fell to the ground. Not only did I fall to the ground, but my knee hit the concrete, too. The scrapes and scratches appeared instantly.

Still trying to process what had happened, I just sat there on the ground, holding my knee and crying. I cried not because of the fall, but because I was allowing myself to go through this stupid cycle, this emotionally and physically draining shit.

I kept my cool, though. I quietly got up and walked into the house. Then I took a shower and went to bed. When I woke up the next morning, Chucky was getting ready to head out the door. I strolled past him and entered the bathroom. As soon as I sat on the toilet, the door flew open, and in walked Chucky.

"I'm about to leave and will be back sometime Sunday. Don't have too much fun, and I will be checking in on you. I love you."

"Me, too," I mumbled.

"'Don't have too much fun,'" I said to myself with a chuckle. I planned on having more fun than I ever had.

I immediately took a shower and got dressed. I put on a long, white and blue fitted dress and some all-white K-Swiss shoes, and I curled my hair. Then I snapped my gold hoop earrings in my ear and shined my lips with some clear lip gloss. After checking myself out in the mirror, I grabbed my blue book bag purse and headed out the door. I was about to hit the streets, but first I had to roll up a blunt. I needed the marijuana to calm my nerves, to feel mellow.

With no destination in mind, I went wherever my car took me. About ten minutes later, my car led me to Garfield Street. As I pulled up to Uncle Skeeter and Aunt Maggie's big white house trimmed in black, I could see they had company over. They were all sitting outside on the porch. I knew I would have a good time and share some laughs, and I could get high because they kept marijuana on deck, and the good stuff, too.

"Hey, boo," Maggie said as I stepped out of the car.

"Hey, Maggie," I replied, also speaking to everyone else on the porch, including my uncle.

"What you up to, Niecy?" my uncle asked while smoking on his blunt.

"Not much, just getting out of the house for a little bit. Needed to get away for a while."

"Where Chucky at? You okay?"

I could see the concern in his eyes.

"He went to Texas with his dad." I rolled my eyes.

I stood there for about twenty more seconds, hoping my uncle did not ask me any more questions about that boy. I was trying to erase him from my mind, at least for the weekend.

Before he could say anything else, I said, "I don't want to talk to him right now."

Everyone on the porch burst out laughing, and my uncle looked at me and threw his hands up as if he were calling a truce.

He then went into his pocket and pulled out a bag of weed and handed it to me. "Roll up then," he grinned.

I took the weed and did exactly that.

Because of his own guilt, I know Chucky Jr. was probably thinking I was going to go out and cheat on him while he was gone, and as bad as I wanted to, I did not cheat. I refused to play the revenge game any longer. I knew he figured I was going to because he was out there cheating with a girl from his job. He thought I did not know, but I knew. A woman has her intuition. Instead of bringing it up, I just played dumb. When I was around the girl, she would act weird, so she told me the truth without actually saying it.

That was one thing I hated about smoking weed. It would have my mind wandering and thinking about all types of shit. Even though I tried not to think about Chucky, his childish actions consumed my mind.

The sound of a big thud interrupted thoughts of me wanting to work on myself. I jumped because the sound startled me, catching me off guard. I looked up and noticed my aunt's friend had fallen. Even though I laughed, I felt bad when I saw the scrapes on her leg. They made me think about my own.

While I enjoyed my time with my family, my body reminded me it was time to head home. I just wanted to go home, put my pajamas on, and find a good movie on TV. I suddenly just wanted to relax. I just wanted to be alone.

♥

As the months rolled by, Chucky Jr. and I began arguing even more. The vibe between us had become so intense. It seemed as if the walls were closing in on me, as if I were dying inside. As if my troubles at home were not enough, I faced some issues at school, too.

On a Wednesday night in December 2000, I was at home sitting on the couch in my Betty Boop nightgown watching *Living Single*. I remember seeing Khadijah, Max, and Regine sneaking into Kyle and Overton's apartment to steal a VHS tape Kyle had of Maxine having sex. Khadijah and Max were looking through the window on the fire escape, one of the funniest scenes in the episode, when my phone rang.

I reluctantly got up from the couch and walked into the dining room to grab the house phone from the dining room table.

"Hello," I said, answering the phone groggily.

"Hey, girl! What you doing?" my friend Tiny asked.

"Nothing, sitting here watching TV, tired as heck."

"Girl, so I heard that Kit wants to fight you, and she and her friends plan on jumping you tomorrow at school," she blurted out.

Sighing, I said, "Tiny, I'm not worried about them, but I appreciate you for calling and telling me. I will be prepared."

After I hung up the phone, I just sat there thinking about what my friend had just told me. I did not understand why Kit had a problem with me. I saw her almost every day inside of school and outside of school. Kit was dating Chucky Jr.'s brother, and this wench had never said anything sideways to me or even acted like she wanted to fight. I could not believe this bitch had my number, knew where I lived, and even had been to my house, but I had to hear from someone else that she had a problem with me. I was so puzzled that the thought of it tickled me.

To ease my mind, I took a Swisher Sweets cigar out of the box, cut it down the middle, emptied the cigar, and filled it with marijuana. I rolled it up, licked the cigar together to make it stick, took the lighter and dried it, and then I set some flame to the end. I inhaled the blunt, held the smoke in, and slowly blew it out, thinking about how the next day was going to play out. This was sure to be interesting.

I woke up feeling anxious the next morning because I did not know who all wanted to jump me. I was still in the dark about how many girls it was going to be and why.

Instead of dressing cute, like I normally did, I threw on some sweats, two T-shirts, and some gym shoes. I put my hair in a ponytail and stuffed a screwdriver in my jacket pocket. I did not want to use the screwdriver, but I intended to use it if I needed to.

When fourth period rolled around, I was in PE. Because that semester of PE was swimming, my class was located across the street at the pool. Kit took the same class, so I could not wait to see how this hour would go.

The class involved a normal day of swimming, except for the last fifteen to twenty minutes of class. I had already changed back into my regular clothes and was sitting in a chair on the side of the pool with a couple of classmates when I heard Kit talking to a couple of other female classmates.

"Yeah, she thinks she is all of that," I heard her annoying voice cackle.

"She is not no trophy," the other girl added.

I was sitting there laughing to myself, thinking, *These bitches are miserable as hell.*

Sammy, the girl I was talking to, said, "So, I guess they about to start with the bullshit?"

I smiled. "Yeah, it looks that way."

"I don't know what she smiling at with her ugly ass." Kit looked directly at me, fuming.

"Bitch, who the fuck you calling ugly with your man-looking ass," I yelled back.

I guess hearing me say she looked like a man hit a nerve because she started yelling, and I stood up and matched her energy. This back-and-forth turned into a screaming match that went on for about five minutes before the swim coach broke us up and sent Kit to the office. When the bell rang, I grabbed my things and headed back across the street to the school.

Fifth period was up next, and I paged for the library during that hour. I restocked books, watched over the library, and assisted the librarian with whatever she needed. As I put some books away, I thought about how badly I needed a blunt to calm myself down and how Kit still had not made her move. I wondered if any of it was worth fighting for. Only Kit knew the answer to that question because I did not have any ill feelings toward her.

A couple of minutes before the bell rang, I saw Danielle, one of my associates from school, walk in as I gathered my things. She wore a concerned look on her face.

"Keren, Kit is outside the library waiting on you," she said.

"Thanks for the heads up."

I grabbed my things and started heading for the door as the bell rang. As soon as I walked out the door, I felt a hit on the left side of my face. That's when the fight popped off. I felt another hit on the right side of my face, but that did not stop me from swinging. I was still fighting with Kit when someone grabbed my arm.

"Keren, your face is bleeding," the voice yelled.

I stopped fighting and took the first white t-shirt off and wiped my face and charged back after Kit with everything inside of me. Two arms came from behind me and scooped me up in mid-air. I was wriggling and kicking, trying to get out of the army recruiter's arms. I noticed Kit running toward the stairs and my brother running after her.

The army recruiter lowered me to the ground and took me by the arm to the office.

"You have to go to the office because your face is bleeding and you need some medical attention," he urged.

I did not speak because I was so shocked and pissed off by what had just happened. I knew she wanted to fight me, but I never thought it was going to go down like that.

By the time I got settled in the office, I noticed an ambulance pulling up to the school. Someone must have called for it before I even reached the office.

"Keren, you have to go to the hospital," Mr. Biersdorf, the school guidance counselor, said.

"I don't want to go to the hospital; I want to kill that bitch," I snapped.

"Keren, please don't say that; there are police around," he advised me.

"I don't give a fuck; I want to kill that bitch," I repeated.

Mr. Biersdorf's eyes searched the room and then landed back on me. "I called your mom, and she is going to meet us at the hospital. I am going to ride with you." He grabbed my hand and led me out of the office as a million thoughts rushed through my head.

On the extremely uncomfortable ride to the hospital, all I could think about was killing that ho. I thought about how I could murder her and get away with it. I even considered the fact that I might get caught and go to jail, but that was a consequence I was willing to suffer because she had to pay.

Once at the hospital, I sat inside a freezing cold hospital room with a white towel up to my face and tears filling my eyes. I looked over at my mom, and she was sitting there trying not to show any concern on her face. I could not blame her, though. The doctor told us I needed to get stitches on both sides of my face: seventeen stitches on one side and twelve on the other side.

I could not believe I now had to live with two big cuts on my face. I went from wanting to model and do fashion shows to looking like Scarface. *How could my life change so quickly? Why would she cut me in my face?* All these questions ran through my head at once, sometimes jumbling together.

Though I was thankful the police had Kit in custody, I was a little annoyed because I wanted my revenge against her. I knew the Lord said, "Vengeance is mine," but I was an impatient person, and I wanted revenge right then and there.

Despite my issues with him, Chucky Jr. tried to be compassionate about what had happened to me. Even though he consoled me in the beginning, it did not last long. Most of the hatred in my heart boiled over to Chucky Jr. and his brother because that was Chucky's brother and his brother's girlfriend, and he was still with her and visiting her in jail. On multiple occasions, I seriously thought about getting my revenge on Kit through Chucky's brother being that he wanted to play "Captain Save-a-Ho".

I talked to Chucky Sr. about the situation, expressing how I felt and admitting all the things I wanted to do. I thought he would try to talk me out of the thoughts that played over and over in my mind, but he simply hugged me.

"Everything is going to be okay; you are still alive and still beautiful," he assured me.

"Thank you, but I feel so ugly, and I want to kill that girl." I could not hide the anger in my voice.

"You want me to bail her out so you can whoop her ass," he chuckled.

I know he was playing, but I considered taking him up on his offer.

Naturally, I did not feel comfortable going back to school right away. I would get panic attacks at the thought of entering that school building. It devastated me that something so violent had happened to me in a place where

I was supposed to feel safe, and I just could not bear the thought of people staring at the scars on my face. At least not while I was so vulnerable and felt so ugly. So I took some time off to get my confidence back, to feel like Keren again.

Being out of school and walking around with stitches on both sides of my face kept me in the house on most days. It gave me more time to be at home with Chucky Jr., and I was not too thrilled about that because I had to see his brother more, and I was still blaming him for the stitches in my face even though he was not the one who hurt me. I also had to make sure I did not get comfortable being at home because it would have been too easy for me to quit school altogether.

After two months of being out of school, I was finally ready to get back into the swing of things. I was ready to complete the next three months and get my diploma. Absolutely nothing could stop me now.

Chapter 11

While I was enjoying a donut with some milk in my second period math class one day, a queasy feeling came over me. I took another sip of my milk and instantly felt like I had to puke. *Maybe I have a bug or something because I'm suddenly not feeling good*, I thought. Seconds later, I grabbed the trash can near the teacher's desk and vomited all over the trash.

What did I eat? I asked myself. I felt so horrible. Because I knew I could not make it the whole day at school, I left and walked to my mom's house, being that I could not contact Chucky Jr. That figures, right?

My mom lived about eight blocks away from the school, and those eight blocks seemed even farther that day. I was so weak from throwing up all morning.

"What are you doing here? Why you not in school?" my mom asked as she closed the door behind me.

"I got sick, and they sent me home. I couldn't get in touch with Chucky, so they allowed me to walk home," I told her.

"What's wrong with you?" she asked with concern in her eyes.

"I don't know. I was in class eating a donut and drinking some milk, and I just started puking." I plopped down on the couch, thankful to have made it there in one piece.

"You might have a stomach bug or something," she told me.

Not thinking much more of it, I climbed into my mom's bed and lay there watching tv until Chucky Jr. came and picked me up.

Because I did not want to wait for a doctor's appointment, I went to the emergency room the next day. I had spent the rest of the day before and all that morning feeling sick.

Once there, the nurse took my vitals and a urine sample. I sat in the hospital room waiting for the doctor to come in and tell me his diagnosis, growing tired and restless because it was taking so long. Having already been there for two hours, I was ready to go home, shower, and get into bed.

Finally, I heard a knock on the door, and the doctor came into the room. With black hair, tan skin, and a medium body frame, he looked to be of middle eastern descent.

"Hello, Karen, my name is Dr. Toriba. How are you doing today?" the doctor said with a foreign accent.

"Besides the upset stomach and puking, I'm okay, I guess," I shrugged.

I sat there on the hospital bed in my hospital gown, looking up at the doctor, anxiously awaiting his diagnosis.

He adjusted his glasses. "Keren, we got your urine sample back and . . . congratulations, Keren. You are pregnant," he said, smiling with his eyes focused on me.

Confusion spread all over my face. “What do you mean, ‘pregnant’?” I asked.

I sat there in shock, trying to process the doctor’s words. I could not believe what I had just heard. As tears ran down my face, I could not believe how I had allowed myself to get pregnant, and by a man who I was ready to end things with. I instantly jumped off the bed and started throwing up in the trash can next to the desk.

It was probably not the best thought at the moment, but I said to myself, *Damn, Keren, you done fucked up now.*

Before I left the hospital, I scheduled an appointment with my doctor for an ultrasound and later found out I was four and a half months pregnant and my due date was September 20th. I did not know what I was having yet, but it was too late to turn back. My baby was coming, and that was something I had to deal with.

I kept my pregnancy a secret from Chucky Jr. and my family until after I went to my ultrasound appointment to confirm I was pregnant. I played out different scenarios of how I would break the news to Chucky in the meantime. Then one day, I just went for it.

“Chucky, I need to talk to you when I get out of school,” I told him as he dropped me off at school one morning.

“Talk about what?” he asked, with a hint of suspicion in his voice.

“It’s nothing bad, but we do need to talk later on,” I assured him.

I wanted to keep my words simple because I did not want the conversation to go left. Though he did not like it, he would have to wait to find out what I needed to talk about.

That day was the only day that school seemed to zoom past. On any other day, a minute seemed like an hour, but now time was working against me. This made me more nervous, but I could not go back on my word.

Before I knew it, 2:25 p.m. had arrived, and the bell rang. It was now the end of the day. I made my way to the first floor where my locker was located. I collected my things and headed outside to wait on Chucky Jr.

All I could think about was, *How in the hell am I going to start this conversation with this boy*? I was so relieved when he started it for me.

"So, what did you need to talk to me about?" Chucky asked as soon as I opened the car door.

"Well, damn. Can you say, 'Hello, how was your day', first," I replied with a hint of sarcasm.

"Hello, how was your day?" He mocked. "What you need to talk about?"

I looked at him and just rolled my eyes. I could not believe his peanut head ass did not care about me; he just wanted to know the topic of the conversation. *Typical ass man*, I thought to myself.

"Well, the day I left school because I was sick . . . you know, the day I had to walk over to my mom's house because you weren't answering your phone?"

He gave me a slight eye roll this time. I just laughed inside and shook my head.

"Like I was saying, the day I left school sick, I went to the hospital, and they told me I'm pregnant. I made an appointment with my doctor, and he confirmed it. I'm pregnant and due September 20th," I explained.

He just sat there staring out the car window, not saying a word. I did not know what to make of his silence, but it was pissing me off.

"Are you going to say anything?" I asked him, pouring the attitude on thick.

"What do you want me to say? It caught me off guard, but I'm not mad about it," he responded.

"Geesh, thanks," I scoffed.

"No, this is just not what I expected. I'm sorry."

Even though his apology surprised me, I would be lying if I said it did not make me feel a little better. The look in his eyes made me think, *Maybe he actually cares.*

"Thank you," I said, trying to savor that moment of peace.

Being that my birthday was coming up, I thought to myself, *What a birthday present this will be.* I was confused, upset, and even disappointed in myself. I kept thinking, *How am I going to go off to school with a baby? How am I going to get away from Chucky with this baby? What am I going to tell my parents?*

In some strange way, behind all the questions and fear were feelings of happiness, excitement, and fulfillment. I still did not want to be with Chucky, but I was thankful he had blessed me with a baby of my own, something I could call mine.

❤

I decided I was going to tell my parents about the baby at the birthday party they were hosting for me. I thought it would be the best timing because my parents would be there and Chucky Sr. would be there, too, making it convenient for them to find out at once.

February 14, 2001 rolled around faster than I had expected. I was now eighteen years old and a mom-to-be. When I walked into my mother's house, I could see red, white, and pink decorations everywhere, keeping with the

Valentine's Day theme. I also spotted a table with a spread of food and a cake just for me. Both my parents were there. My cousin Chrissy and her husband had come from Indiana to attend the party. Chucky Sr. and his girlfriend were there, too, and even Chucky's brother had shown up.

Shouts of "Happy Birthday" were all I heard as I walked through the house.

My stepdad approached me first, giving me a hug. "Happy Birthday," he said.

"Thank you, and thank you guys for the party," I replied gratefully.

Next, I walked over to Chucky Sr. and gave him a hug. "Happy Birthday, Keren," he said. He motioned to pin some money onto my shirt.

"Thank you, Chucky. I appreciate you." My face beamed. I would have held onto him longer had I known that would be the last time I would hug him.

"Happy Birthday! You want some of this wine cooler?" my cousin Chrissy asked.

"Thank you, and no thank you." I waved off her offer.

"It's your birthday. Have a drink," she urged.

"I'm good," I chuckled.

Well, I guess this would be the perfect time to tell everyone since Chrissy is harassing me about having a drink.

"Hey, everybody! Hey," I yelled across the room.

I looked over at my mom. "Can you turn the music down real quick?"

Even though the music was not loud, I wanted complete silence when I told everyone the news.

"First, I want to thank you all for helping me celebrate my birthday. I appreciate each and every one of you." I paused and then exhaled. "I hadn't been feeling too good, so I went to the doctor, and I was told that I am pregnant, and the baby will be born in September."

I exhaled again, thinking, *Okay, it's out now*, but I was afraid to hear everyone's responses, especially my parents.

"Congratulations," they all said.

Surprisingly, they all were cool with it. Isn't it funny how your own mind can play games with you?

One by one, they walked up to me and touched my stomach. I was glad that everything was finally out in the open and I could start taking care of me and my baby. I was ready to become this child's mommy and to start planning my future, but not before I tackled school first.

♥

It was a little over a month later when I received one of the worst calls in my life. I had gotten out of school and was standing outside waiting for Chucky Jr. to pick me up, but he was already late. I instantly got pissed because I was standing there holding a few books that were weighing my arm down. Growing tired of waiting, I called Chucky, but his phone kept going to voicemail. The more I dialed his number, the more irritated I became. *Why the hell is he not answering his phone*, I thought to myself. *The bastard is probably out with that bitch.*

I sat outside of the school for forty minutes before I walked up the street to my grandma's house. As I walked, the people I passed on the street could probably feel the heat coming from my body. I was a raging bull, ready to pounce.

When I arrived at my grandmother's house, her door was open, so I opened the screen door and walked in.

As soon as she saw me, she said, "Chucky just called here looking for you."

"Why the heck is he calling here when I have been calling him for the past hour, wondering where the heck he was?" I replied. "Did he say anything?"

"No, he just said to tell you he called."

As she ended her sentence, my phone rang. I looked inside of my purse and pulled out my cell phone. I flipped it open and answered it.

"Hello?"

"Where are you at?" I heard a male voice on the other line, and I automatically knew who it was.

"I'm at my grandma's house. I just got here." I told him. "Where are you at?"

"I'm on my way to pick you up," Chucky replied with sadness in his voice.

I could hear that something was wrong with him. His voice was cracking, and I could tell he had been crying. I replaced the frustration in my voice with concern.

"What's wrong? Are you okay, Chucky?" I asked.

"No, Keren. My dad is dead," he sobbed loudly.

"Oh my gosh, babe. I'm so sorry. What happened?" I sobbed with him.

"I can't talk right now. I'll be there shortly."

I hung up the phone and broke down. I shed so many tears. My heart dropped to my stomach. My chest started getting tighter, and it was becoming hard for me to breathe. I could not believe this was happening. I had so many questions in my head, so many thoughts.

Almost forgetting where I was, I felt my grandma's arm wrap around me, and she handed me some Kleenex. She helped pick me up off the floor and guided me over to the couch.

"What's wrong?" she asked, still holding me in her arms.

"That was Chucky Jr. on the phone. He just told me that Chucky Sr. is dead," I sobbed, barely getting the words out of my mouth.

"What happened?" she asked.

"I don't know. He didn't tell me. He is on his way to pick me up."

My grandma rose from the couch and went to the bathroom to grab more Kleenex. I was still sitting there, crying uncontrollably. Just when my grandma entered the living room and handed me the tissues, I heard a car horn blowing outside. I got up and went to the door. Noticing it was Chucky Jr., I immediately turned around and gathered my things.

"I'll see you later, Grandma," I said before exiting her house.

"Make sure you call me and let me know how you are doing," she called out after me.

I got in the car and reached out my arms to hug Chucky. At that moment, I just wanted to hold him and let him know I was there for him. He laid his head in my arms and just cried. I really did not know what to say because I had never been in his position before.

"I am so sorry, Chucky, but I promise I will be here for you. I have your back, and we will get through this together," I assured him.

He did not respond, but I knew he was thankful. I also knew he could not talk because he was still in shock and could not process anything at the moment.

It seemed as if my heart shattered when Chucky told me his dad, Mr. Chucky Sr., had passed away. His death hit me hard. It was one of the hardest things I had to endure. It was as if I had lost my best friend. Chucky Sr. had always been there for me. I could call him about anything, and he would be there for me, and with no judgment. I often wondered, *How am I going to do this without him?* He was truly a big part of my support system, and I was going to miss him dearly. He would always hold a spot in my heart, and I would always have nothing but love for him.

The one thing I hated most about this tragedy was that my child would never get the chance to meet her grandfather, and Chucky Sr. would never meet his grandchild.

♥

With Chucky Sr. gone, I knew I would be on my own with the Chucky Jr. situation. I knew I would have no one to talk to or anyone to give me real advice. I also knew I was going to get my diploma in honor of Chucky Sr. I was going to make something out of myself, and I was going to get away from Chucky Jr. by any means necessary.

To get caught up with my schoolwork and graduate with my class, I had to take some night school classes at the adult education school. Even though I received my homework when I missed school, I still missed some assignments that were a huge part of my grades. So I had one of two choices: either go to night school or not graduate. Classes lasted about three hours a night, but it was only two nights a week for one month.

I shared night school classes with my cousin Keisha, which made things much easier for me because I had someone to talk to and to help me with my assignments. Keisha was the same age as me. Her birthday was three days after mine, and we were pretty close. We had been that way ever since we were little girls. Keisha was my uncle Jimmy's and step-aunt Lisa's daughter. I could talk to her about anything, even the grief and joy I felt all at the same time.

♥

On April 15, 2001, I left school early because I had a doctor's appointment to find out the sex of my baby. Chucky Jr. had picked me up from school to attend the appointment with me. Though I had a little bump, I was still not showing, so I kept the pregnancy a secret from plenty of people, including friends, for a while longer.

I lay on the hospital bed in my hospital gown, waiting for the nurse and doctor to return to the room and get the process started. Chucky sat in the chair next to the doctor's desk. He was sitting there messing with his phone, probably texting the chick he had been messing around with.

"Are you excited?" I asked, trying to steal some of his attention.

"I'm cool," he replied, still focused on his phone.

I smacked my lips. "Why did you even come?"

While I did not want to be a pain in the butt, his attitude and verbal abuse had worsened since his father's death. I knew Chucky Jr. was still trying to process it because it had only been a month, but I also thought he would have gotten his act together. I thought that maybe his father's death would have been a wake-up call and that he would have taken having another child as a blessing. Chucky Jr. already had a daughter with another girl; she was pregnant when I first met him. The funny thing is, the girl and I actually knew each other and were good friends in middle school.

How I saw it, one life was taken but one was also given. That is what I focused on. It helped me cope with the pain.

"Keren, now is not the time, okay?" he growled.

I just stared at him. I did not press any further because I did not want us to argue in the doctor's office.

Seconds later, a knock came across the door, bringing me back to the reason for my visit. I looked up, and the doctor was poking his head in.

"Is it okay to come in?" the doctor asked.

"Yes, let's get this over with," I said, trying to sound anxious yet a little annoyed.

"Okay, I need you to lay on back, put this cover over you, and lift your gown up," he said. "This is going to be a little warm."

He put some blue gel on his gadget and rubbed it across my stomach. I was watching the monitor and could see the outline of my baby. Seeing my baby made me feel so proud. I looked over at Chucky, and he was still doing something on his phone. I shook my head and shed a couple of tears because even though he was there, I felt so alone.

I shifted my concern to my baby when I heard the doctor's voice.

"Well, Keren, it looks like you are going to be having a baby girl," he said with a wide grin on his face, like he was delivering the best news ever.

"Really? Are you sure?" I asked, hoping for a different outcome.

"I am quite sure, dear. I see a hamburger, not a hotdog," he replied. "You sound disappointed."

"No, not disappointed, but I did want a boy."

"What about you, Dad?" the doctor asked Chucky.

Chucky looked up long enough to reply to the doctor. "I'm okay with whatever," he replied.

The doctor took his eyes off Chucky and directed them back to me. "You want to hear the heartbeat?"

"Yes, of course," I said.

First, there was silence. Then I heard the most beautiful sound ever. Hearing my baby's heartbeat sent a chill over my body. I could not believe I had something growing inside of me and it had a heartbeat. Seeing her and hearing her heartbeat put me in a content and peaceful mood. I was going to love my daughter with everything inside of me. I was going to be the best mom I could be.

♥

A month later, on May 15, 2001, it was my graduation day. I wore a long flower dress underneath my graduation cap and gown. The overcrowded gym held everyone's friends and family, and it was extremely hot. Being that I was five months pregnant, I was annoyed and ready to get out of there. However, none of that mattered when I heard my name being called.

When I held my diploma in my hand, I realized I had finally done it. It took a lot of work, and I had experienced some troubled times, but I had made it. I was officially a high school graduate. This was a major accomplishment for me, and I was so proud of myself for not giving up, for pushing and fighting to make it through it. I knew I could not let my parents down, or Chucky Sr. My parents were so excited for me, and they were so proud that I had finished school. They were in attendance along with Chucky Jr., my mom's oldest brother, and my siblings.

"I did this one for you, Chucky Sr.! Here is my diploma!"

I shouted those exact words when I took my diploma up to the wall where Chucky Sr. was buried. I was so sad that he could not be there, but I was happy that I had done it, and that was all he wanted me to do: finish school.

Yes, y'all, I did it! Just like he believed I would.

Chapter 12

After no longer being held hostage by high school, it was time for me to make a major life decision. I had a daughter on the way and a brand-new set of responsibilities.

At the beginning of September 2001, four months after my graduation and a couple of weeks before my baby's due date, Chucky and I moved into a new two-bedroom apartment to make room for our child. Shortly after, I set up the baby's room, and I even prepared my hospital bag for when I went into labor.

On September 7th, I started having contractions. The pain was extreme. I was lying down in the bedroom watching *Law and Order* when the contractions began. I was all into the show, too. The wife of this woman's lover had killed a lady, and all the evidence pointed toward the lover because the wife was setting the husband up. I forgot all about the show when those pains kicked in.

"Chuuckyyy!" I screamed in between bursts of pain.

"What?" he answered.

"I'm having shots of pain. I think I'm having contractions."

By the time Chucky came into the bedroom, I was curled up into a fetal position with tears streaming down my face. The pain was worse than menstrual cramps. It felt like someone had a hold on my insides and was squeezing with every bit of their strength.

Not even three hours before, the doctors had sent me home from the hospital after telling me I was not in labor. Now, the pain was getting stronger, and the contractions were coming more frequently.

"What's wrong with you?" Chucky asked, as if it irritated him to check on me.

"I'm hurting," I said, thinking it was quite obvious what was wrong.

"Why don't you try and take a shower? Maybe it will make you feel better," he said.

I thought that was the most ridiculous thing anyone could say. How in the hell was a shower going to take this pain away? And how in the hell would I be able to stand long enough to take a shower? I could barely move. I did not have the strength to argue with him, so I just dragged myself to the bathroom to hop into the shower.

Barely able to grip the knob because of my trembling hands, I turned the hot water on and climbed in. I tried letting the water run down my body, but the pain was too excruciating. I just wanted to lie back down and ball up.

I damn near crawled out of the bathroom and ended up on our bedroom floor. I curled up until the contraction stopped and then yelled, "Chuckyyyy!"

"Yeah?" he yelled back.

"I need to go back to the hospital," I cried to him.

"Keren, we just came from the hospital. They said you were not in labor. I'm not going back up there and sitting that long for them to send you home again."

"How you gone tell me what the hell is going on with my body? I said I need to go to the fucking hospital, and I need to go now. Either you are going to take me, or I can call my mom, but I'm going to that fucking hospital," I snapped.

"Well, would you like to put some clothes on?" he asked sarcastically.

I did not have time for the back and forth. I just wanted to get to the hospital, but if I could have, I would have punched the shit out of him right then and there.

When I finally arrived at the hospital, the staff admitted me immediately. *I fucking knew it*, I thought to myself. They wheeled me up to the labor and delivery floor. The doctor came in and examined me to see how much I had dilated.

"You've dilated to a 4," the doctor said.

That's it?

Honestly, I thought the process would be quick. I thought I would just go in there and deliver my baby, and it would be over in record time, but that is not how it went. Just because I was dilating did not mean I was ready to have the baby. I had to wait to be dilated more, and to see if my water had broken.

Finally, the time arrived. I delivered my baby the next day on September 8, 2001. I gave birth to a beautiful baby girl, whom I named Charity. Chucky Jr. and my cousin Kendra, my uncle Jimmy's stepdaughter, helped me name her.

Giving birth to my daughter was the most amazing feeling in the world. This little person had come from my body. I had given her life, and little did she know, she had given me life, too. I could not believe I was someone's mommy.

♥

You would think having a baby would bring you and your significant other closer together, that you would have a bond between the two of you that could not be explained or broken. But with my relationship with Chucky Jr., that was not the case. It was as if he and I had become more distant since my daughter's birth. Chucky would leave me at home alone with the baby, and he would be in the streets doing God knows what with God knows who. Our arguments became more intense, and instead of being a team, we were like enemies. Or at least that's how I felt.

Not only did the arguments become more frequent, but the cheating also became more obvious. Chucky would come home all hours of the night after being gone all day. There was no doubt in my mind he was with the girl from his job.

One Friday night, we were sitting in the living room of our apartment—well my apartment because the lease was in my name—watching *The Wayans Bros* when a knock sounded at the front door. Because I was rocking Charity to sleep, I did not get up to answer the door.

"Can you get the door?" I asked Chucky.

As Chucky got up and walked to the door, I put Charity down and peeped out the window. There was a white car parked in front of our apartment; the headlights were off, but the park lights were on.

"Who is it?" he called out.

I looked toward the door and noticed he had cracked the door wide enough for him to peek out, and then he shut the door back. Even though he closed the door quickly, I caught a glimpse of a woman.

"You have the wrong house," he spoke through the closed door.

He walked back to the couch and sat down like nothing was going on, but I could tell something was not right by the "Oh shit, I'm busted" look he wore on his face.

"Who was that?" I asked him.

"They were looking for my brother," he replied, fidgeting like he feared getting caught in his lie.

Oh, so this muthafucka thinks I'm slow as hell. This nigga really thinks he's slick.

"Why would you tell them they had the wrong house instead of saying your brother doesn't live here?" I asked him. "That doesn't make sense."

"Don't start, Keren," he said.

"Yeah, nigga, you think you slick. I saw that white car out there. Same damn car that ol' girl at your job drive," I yelled.

"There you go with that insecure shit again. Just because you see a car like hers doesn't mean it was hers. They didn't make one car and stop," he yelled back.

"Bitch, if I'm insecure, it's because of your dumb ass!" I continued screaming at him. "You got bitches coming to my house looking for you. You a disrespectful ass nigga!"

"I don't have time to argue with you. I have to go and get my uncle from work," he said.

"I bet yo' ass do," I responded before hearing the door slam.

Chucky left the house at 11:15 p.m. I was sitting there pissed off and crying, wondering why I was going through this bullshit. I knew I deserved better than what he was offering, and I knew I could do better, but I just could not muster up the strength to leave. Still, I knew this had to be the last straw.

I rolled up a blunt, put my child in her bassinet, and sat on that couch in the dark crying, waiting for Chucky to walk through the door.

The things I allowed Chucky Jr. to put me through had drained my soul. I was dealing with postpartum depression and a no-good-ass nigga, so it seemed as if I did not stand a chance. The postpartum depression had me feeling so down, not wanting to do anything, always feeling tired. I did not want to get out of bed, and I did not want to be bothered. I did not even want to hold my child most days. I felt like I was just existing physically while feeling dead emotionally and mentally. I was ready to go.

How could I end this? I asked myself as I continued sitting on the couch that night. *How could I make it painless and quick?* I figured pills would be the answer. I was going to use pills to end my life.

I got up to walk upstairs to the medicine cabinet when I heard the front door open. Chucky walked through the door slowly, trying to be quiet. I just stood on the stairs, watching him fiddle around with the lock. Even though I wanted to swing on him, I did not have the strength. I walked down the stairs and looked at the stove for the time. It was 2:30 in the damn morning, and his ass wanted to stroll through like he had it like that.

Completely exhausted, I walked back down the stairs and lay on the couch. I did not want to be near him at all. He did not care, though. I knew he would not care because he had gotten his fix from his little girlfriend. I lay there in a fetal position asking God, "Why me? What have

I done so wrong for me to go through what I am going through?" I told God I needed her and needed her to help me with this situation. I needed the strength to leave. Desperately, I cried, prayed, and begged for her help.

As I held the bottle of pills in my hand with the lid off, I thought, *This is it*. I was finally about to do it, but I felt something hovering around me. I cannot say what it was, but I felt a presence around me. It felt like a hand grabbed my hand and threw the bottle of pills. The bottle hit the wall and bounced onto the floor, spilling pills all over it. All I could do was cry. I cried so much that I cried myself to sleep.

The next day, I awoke to Chucky bringing me Charity and him walking out the door. I did not ask any questions, and I really did not care. Even though I did not know it then, that day would welcome my escape from Chucky.

I had just put Charity down for a nap, so I was going to enjoy some me time. I rolled myself a blunt and poured myself a glass of wine. No, I was not of the legal age to drink, but for someone who had experienced childbirth, postpartum depression, mental abuse, cheating, lying, and suicidal thoughts, I believed I deserved a glass of wine. Chucky was of age, so he had bought the wine for me a few days prior.

With my wineglass in hand, I sat down at the dining room table that I loved so much—Chucky Sr.'s table—and began writing. Writing helped me clear my mind. It helped me release all the anger and pain I held inside. It gave me peace of mind. A sense of comfort.

I was still sitting there when I heard my front door being unlocked. I did not even turn my head because I knew it had to be Chucky Jr. Being that I did not care to see him, I remained focused on writing out my thoughts.

"What you doing?" I heard Chucky Jr. say in a low, somewhat compassionate voice.

Hmm, he's acting like he cares, so he either wants something or knows I am truly fed up with his ass and wants to get back in my good graces.

"Writing and smoking," I replied to him, stating the obvious.

"Well, I wanted to talk to you. Do you have a couple minutes to spare?" he asked while looking over my shoulders. I could feel his breath on my neck.

I sucked my teeth hard and rolled my eyes as I turned around to face him.

"What's up?"

"I've been talking to my mom, and she wants to move to Georgia, and I plan on moving with her."

I sat there listening to him with not one ounce of care, but I had to act like I did care to avoid starting an argument. I was actually happy and grateful that God had finally answered my prayers.

Like a pro, I turned on the dramatics. "So you just had a newborn baby, and you plan on leaving her and moving to Georgia?"

"I'm sorry, but I have to do this for me, Keren. I still can be her dad from Georgia," he said.

"So that's it for us?"

"I think it's best that we go our separate ways and see other people."

Hell yeah, I thought, but I could not say that without seeming too anxious. So, I played it cool.

"Okay, Chucky, whatever you want," I responded, trying to sound as settled as possible.

"Are you cool with this?" he asked me.

Of course, nigga. I took a long pull off my blunt. *You done made my day for real.*

"I have no choice," I said aloud, taking another pull and passing the blunt to him.

"We will be leaving in about a week," he told me, with a blank stare on his face.

"Oh, so soon?" I asked.

"Yeah, Mom wants to leave as soon as possible."

Well damn, is she on the run? I laughed to myself.

All I could say was, "Okay."

♥

Exactly a week later, Chucky was knocking at my door. I had not seen him since the day we talked, and I must admit, it took some getting used to, but life was very peaceful. I did not have to worry about arguing, fighting, or wondering if he was cheating. I was in a good place and loving it.

I opened the door to find Chucky standing there, looking like a lost puppy.

"Can I help you?" I asked him through the screen door.

"Keren, I just want to see my baby before I leave. Can I see Charity?" he asked me.

Even though I did not want him back in the house, I would never keep him from seeing his child, so I allowed him to spend some time with Charity. The whole time he was there, he was in the living room, and I was in the kitchen sitting at the dining room table, minding my own business.

Before Chucky Jr. made his departure, he kissed his daughter and put her in her swing. When he walked out the door, I knew that would be the end of us as a couple or anything close to it. No discussions about anything other than our child. No booty calls. No sneaky links. NO NOTHING. That chapter was closed.

I thought of Chucky Jr. leaving as a blessing from God. I had cried so many nights and begged so many days for guidance and strength, and for a way out. The morning after I wanted to commit suicide, he came home and told me he was moving, so it could have been nothing but God or my ancestors, maybe a little of both. Regardless, it was a blessing for sure.

Though I was quite unsure where my life would lead me after this chapter of my life, I knew I was going to make the best of this new path. I needed some freedom, some fun, and some comfort, and I knew exactly how to get that.

I hopped on the phone and called Sabrina, Chucky Jr.'s cousin. She was the only person I really vibed with besides her brother, E. Sabrina was way older than me, but she knew how to party, and she had a newborn, too. Our babies were only two months apart, if that much.

"Hello," Sabrina said as she answered the phone.

"Hey, boo. What you doing?"

"Girl, nothing . . . sitting here bored as hell.

"Well, you know me and Chucky are no longer; he and your auntie moved to Georgia, and I am ready to have some fun. I need to get out and kick it."

"We can do that; I'm with it."

"I'll call my cousins and see if they can come over and babysit," I said, excited beyond belief.

"Okay, cool. Let them know. I will hook them up," she said.

"Alright, I'll holler."

Immediately, I called my two younger cousins over to the house so that they could babysit the kids. We needed both of them because they would be watching two newborns. As a thank you for their help, we would give them a couple of dollars and some drinks and keep them stocked with weed.

Sabrina and I went to one of the local bars to celebrate my newfound freedom. We drank Jose Cuervo Gold while shooting some darts. And yes, I imagined Chucky's face as the target a few times.

I woke up the next morning feeling like crap from a hangover—tequila had won that round—but feeling so good because I was doing what I wanted to do, and I had no one to answer to.

As I sat on the toilet with a headache and a nauseous stomach, I thought, *Last night was one of the best nights of my life.* I enjoyed the feeling of being free and feeling accepted. This feeling was new to me, and I loved it. I refused to let it ever leave me.

Chapter 13

Once Chucky Jr. was out of the picture, I began seeing Brian. Brian was Sabrina's cousin on her mom's side. I had been around him before when I was still with Chucky, but we stopped hanging around him because Chucky did not like the way Brian used to look at me. Now that I was single and ready to mingle, I wanted to see what Brian was all about.

Brian was a light-skinned guy, really light-skinned. He was a Kevin Gates type of guy. He wore a short haircut and had a medium build, and he even had gold teeth in his mouth. Brian was not someone I would normally go for, but my normal was not working. I figured it would not hurt to try something different.

Like most dudes, Brian said he did not have a girlfriend, but I knew he was still entertaining his ex. Even though I was unsure if they were together, I was certain they were still messing around. I did not care, though. She was not my friend, and he was not my man. I owed no one any loyalty, respect, or explanation.

After being single for only a month, I learned a certain someone was trying to disrupt my plans. I was sitting in my living room one day, not giving Chucky Jr. a thought. I had just showered, and I was in total relaxation mode. With just shorts and a tank top on, I rolled a blunt and poured a shot of Jose Cuervo tequila as R. Kelly played in the background. The only visible light was from the kitchen. But as soon as I was ready to get in my mood, my home phone rang.

I did not have a caller ID, so I answered it blindly. "Hello?"

"Hey, Keren," I heard a familiar voice say.

Instantly, a shot of pain went down my spine and around to my stomach. I knew exactly who it was, but I did not know what he wanted.

"Hey, what's up?" I asked, not really caring but curious to know what Chucky Jr. was calling for.

"I just wanted to let you know that me and Mom are moving back to Illinois. We came down here thinking it was going to be good living, but we have been living foul."

I sat there quietly, just listening to him talk and wondering why he was telling me this. I did not care how they were living. They were both grown, and if that is what they wanted, then so be it.

He continued on to say, ". . . the place we been staying at has roaches, and some nights we have been sleeping in the car."

I continued sitting there quietly, waiting for him to finish before I said anything.

"Well, if you guys are living like that, maybe y'all should move back. That's no way for anyone to live," I told him.

Even though I told him that, in no way did I want him back, nor was it possible for him to come back to *my* house. *Those days are over, and I am not going back*, I said to myself.

"We will be leaving here in the next couple of days," he responded.

"Okay, you guys have safe travels."

I hung up the phone a little pissed, thinking, *This nigga just messed my whole mood up with this bullshit*. I fired up my blunt and thought about the conversation some more. *Some nerve*, I said to myself.

After Chucky Jr.'s little stunt, Sabrina came over to my house with an ounce of weed, some Swisher Sweets cigars, and some tequila. She had her hair styled in a fake ponytail, wearing some jeans, black clog boots, and a cute blouse. Based on her appearance alone, I knew she wanted to go out.

"Girl, throw some clothes on and let's go down to The Legion. Matt done pissed me off," she ranted while handing me the blunt.

Matt was her boyfriend and the father of her newborn daughter. The Legion was a bar the older crowd frequented, but they did not card—check IDs—at the door, so I could sneak my young ass up in there with no problem.

"I don't have time for his shit tonight. That's why I clipped some weed from his ass," she said, inhaling the smoke.

"I sure could use a night out. Girl," I said, pausing for a dramatic effect. "Chucky just called and said he and his momma are moving back to Illinois."

"What the fuck for?" Sabrina looked me straight in the eyes. "I know you better not be thinking about getting back with his ass."

"Girl, naw, I'm not going back," I assured her.

"Awe shit, it's probably gone be some shit between Chucky and Brian," she smirked and shook her head.

I scoffed. "I hope not. I don't have time for any drama. I'm not neither one of theirs, so they can keep whatever might transpire to themselves," I sassed.

The situationship between Brian and me was nothing serious. I knew Brian was all the way bad for me, but I did not want to stop messing with him, and I was not going to stop until I was ready to stop. I knew we would never be together, and it was not because he did not want to be with me. I did not want to be with him. It was a convenience thing. He was helping me get over Chucky. He was a rebound. That's it. That's all.

After pushing the conversation with Chucky to the back of my mind, I tagged along with Sabrina to the Legion. There were only a handful of people in the building that night. Though it was usually packed, I was okay with the small crowd because I did not feel like being around too many people.

After Sabrina and I ordered our drinks, we exchanged our dollars for some quarters to throw darts. We had not even been there twenty minutes when I looked toward the front door and spotted Kandy walking in. Kandy was the girl Brian used to be in a relationship with, the girl whom he said he was not with anymore. I sighed heavily because I knew it was about to be a shit of a night.

Damn, here we go, I thought to myself, refusing to allow her presence to affect my demeanor. I would never let her see me sweat, nor would I ever let her see me show my emotions. I did not even know for sure if she knew I was talking to Brian.

"Are you cool?" Sabrina asked when she noticed Kandy in the club.

"Yeah, I'm good," I replied with a chuckle.

I turned my drink up and picked my darts up to take my turn on the dartboard. As I stood there pointing the dart toward the target, out of the corner of my eye, I saw Kandy walking over to where Sabrina and I stood. I smirked because I knew where this was about to go.

"Hey, Sabrina," Kandy said.

I was still at the line about to throw my second dart, acting like I was not paying attention to them, but I sure as hell was all ears.

"What's up, Kandy?" I heard Sabrina respond.

"Hey, Keren," I heard Kandy call out to me.

Is this wench being sincere, or is this wench trying to be funny? Responding with actions instead of words, I gave her the head nod and threw my third and final dart.

I pulled my darts out of the target and walked back to the table where we were sitting. Then I sat my darts down and picked up my drink. Before I could even turn it up, I heard some crazy words fly out of Kandy's mouth.

"Are you and Brian messing around?" she asked me.

Well, well, well. I knew the "hi" wasn't sincere. I see the true motive now.

"What did Brian tell you, Kandy?" I asked.

"He told me that y'all just cool," she responded.

"Well, that's what it is then."

No, I was not being completely honest. Even though Brian and I *were* cool, we were also messing around. But I felt as if she should have been taking that up with him and not me. He was the one who owed her an explanation, not me.

"So, you just gone sit here in my face and fucking lie to me," she said, the aggression heavy in her voice.

I honestly was trying to play it cool, but this girl was really starting to piss me off. She was questioning me about *her* nigga. Not to mention, she was ruining my high.

"Hold the fuck up! Who the hell you talking to?" I asked her, losing my patience.

"How are you gone mess with him knowing we're together?" she asked, better yet demanded.

"Listen here, Kandy. Yes, I knew you guys were messing around. Together? No, I didn't know because he said you two are not a thing, but that is not my business. I am not your girl, and I owe you nothing. Any questions, concerns, fears, whatever need to be between you and that lying ass nigga of yours. I don't have time for y'all shit." My voice boomed over the noise.

I was waiting for her to get smart or to keep going because I was prepared to hurt her feelings by telling her everything: everything we did and everything he said about her. I was not a cold-hearted ass person, but I was sick of this topic. All I wanted to do was finish my drink and game, but that was not about to happen.

"Kandy, you need to handle that with Brian," Sabrina interjected in a calm and neutral tone. "This is not the time or the place."

I could not believe this girl had the nerve to come at me about *her* lying ass nigga. She was coming at me like she was really hard. I chuckled and then tossed my drink back. *This shit is funny as hell.*

"Keren, let's go before they call the police and you get in trouble because you are underage in here," Sabrina urged.

With no rebuttal, I killed my drink and headed for the door with my head held high, a smile on my face, and a stroll out of this world. I wanted to make sure Kandy saw the way I was so unbothered by her. I even did the white-girl hair flip as I walked out. While I usually would not be so petty, this girl had shown me her emotions, and I was going to play on them. Childish? Yes, I know, but what can I say? I was young and dumb. This girl, well lady, was at least ten years older than me.

♥

After my encounter with Kandy at The Legion, there was bad blood between us. It always amazed me how women would argue and fight over a man when they should have actually come together and double-teamed his ass and left him alone. But I guess that only happened on TV.

I did not have any personal beef with Kandy until she started popping up at my house, looking for her nigga. That was where she crossed the line. I did not even care about her popping up at the hotel or following us, but my philosophy was, keep that shit in the streets. Do not bring it to my house.

So, I know y'all are probably thinking, *This girl popped up at the hotel and followed y'all?* Let me explain.

On the day before my nineteenth birthday in February 2002, I was at home having a drink and smoking a blunt when I heard my phone ring.

"Hello," I said, blowing smoke out of my mouth.

"What you doing?"

I did not have to ask who it was because I recognized Brian's voice.

"Sitting here smoking me a blunt and having a drink. I was about to start cooking." I tried to make the cooking part sound sexy so that he could say, "I'm on my way."

"Don't bother. I'll be over there in about thirty minutes, so be dressed and ready to go."

"Go where?"

"Don't worry about it. Just do as I said."

Usually, I would have gotten smart with his ass, but that shit kind of turned me on. Feeling a little excited down below, I just smiled and said, "Okay."

Eager to get the night started, I passed my cousin the blunt, turned the music up a notch, and ran upstairs to shower. I covered my body in a long-sleeved black dress that hugged my frame like a glove. I finally had my body back. After giving birth to Charity, I had lost all my baby weight and then some. She took all my weight; I weighed probably 125, if that.

Adding a few finishing touches, I put some curls in my hair, sprayed my perfume all over, and put on my jewelry. I was ready.

The phone rang again and, of course, I knew who it was before I even answered it.

"Hello," I answered.

"Come on outside."

I walked outside, and there Brian stood next to a white limousine. I smiled instantly as I watched him open the door.

"Come on," he called out to me.

I climbed into the limo and noticed he had someone he knew driving it. He even had the limo stocked with liquor and three of his friends chilling inside. While I scoped everything out, Brian went into the house and told one of my cousins to come on. The other one had to stay and babysit because she was not old enough to party with us.

For two hours, we rode around listening to music, drinking, smoking, and talking. I would have loved for it to be just the two of us, but it was cool because I knew everyone and we were all cool with each other. My birthday was only hours away, and I just wanted to have fun.

After our time was up, we dropped off my cousin and Brian's friend, Tim, at my apartment. Brian and I got dropped off at Brian's truck. His maroon Expedition sat parked at one of his friends' houses.

Taking off in his truck, we headed to the gas station so that I could get a cup of ice and some Swishers before we dropped his other friend off and headed to the hotel. Brian told me we would be staying at the hotel that night because he wanted us to have some privacy.

We were driving down University Street when Brian's friend, who was sitting in the back of the truck, said, "Brian, someone is behind you flashing their lights."

I turned around and noticed a car driving fast behind us and flashing its lights. Watching the side of Brian's head, I asked, "Who is it?"

"I don't know; I can't see," he said.

The car pulled up on the side of us, speeding like a bat out of hell and then jumping back behind us to avoid the oncoming traffic.

"Brian, I believe it's your girl," his friend said.

"What the hell is she doing?" Brian asked, looking puzzled.

"Evidently trying to get your attention," I popped off with my smart-ass mouth.

I turned and looked in the back again and burst out laughing because I had never been in a car chase before. It was mind-blowing to see the measures we women go through over a man.

He's cool and all, but I mean, he is not all that. I definitely can't see myself going through these measures over his ass, I thought.

"So, you're not going to pull over," I asked Brian sarcastically.

Brian just turned his head and looked at me, but he did not reply. I knew that look screamed "I'm not in the mood". I just sat back in the seat and continued to laugh inside.

A few minutes later, I noticed Brian speeding up and turning corners quickly, trying to lose her. They played this game for about ten minutes before he finally lost her. By then, the chase had already lost its amusement and had become extremely annoying because my night was being ruined.

After what seemed like an eternity, Brian dropped his friend off, and we went to the hotel. I rolled me a blunt, smoked it, and crashed. I hope he did not think he was going to get any that night, not after the drama he had just put me through. It was not happening . . . at all.

The next morning, we awoke to the hotel phone ringing. The first time, neither one of us answered, but the phone started ringing again. Brian rolled over and answered the phone.

"Hello," he answered, all groggy and sleepy.

I was unsure who was on the other line, but he immediately jumped up and ran to the window. He was all hysterical, trying to put his clothes on and hurry outside. As Brian flew out the door, I ran to the window. I pulled the curtain back and spotted Kandy sitting in the driver's seat of Brian's truck. I shook my head and smiled. When she just so happened to look up, I just so happened to wave at her. Okay, maybe I did it on purpose.

For ten minutes, I watched them as they stood there arguing; I assumed. From their body language, I knew the conversation was not a friendly one.

Soon, boredom set in, so I rolled up a blunt and poured myself a drink. *It's five o'clock somewhere,* I thought to myself. It was my birthday, and I was about to enjoy every minute of it, either with or without Brian.

I do not know what Brian said to that crazy lady, but she finally left after about half an hour. We left the hotel shortly after.

"I will see you later, Keren," Brian said when he pulled up to my crib.

"Okay." Translation: "Yeah, right."

"No, you will see me. It's your birthday, and we gone kick it."

Again, I said, "Okay."

"Happy Birthday," he said, finally.

"Thank you," I replied as I hopped out of the truck.

I closed the door and walked into my apartment, thinking, *This nigga not coming back.*

Yes, I saw Brian that night, but it was late that night. His ass showed up after ten. I knew he had to do some making up with Kandy, but I did not even care because I still enjoyed my day with my cousins, my girl Sabrina, and his friend Tim. I was not in the mood to let him or Kandy spoil my high.

When he came in, I was already drunk. The tequila had me horny, so all I wanted Brian to do was sex me and put me to bed.

The next morning, I thought I was dreaming when I heard a horn honking repeatedly. I lay there thinking, *I wish they would go to the door and stop honking that damn horn.*

"It's too dang early for that shit," I said to myself.

I got up and looked out my bedroom window and thought, *Here we go again.* Kandy was outside my apartment. I opened my window and stuck my head out.

"Kandy, what the fuck do you want?" I yelled.

"Where is Brian? Is he here?" she asked me.

"Why the hell are you at my house looking for his ass?" I replied.

"Send him out because I know he's here. I saw his car around the corner."

Damn, this girl has serious issues. She needs to be a detective.

I turned to look at Brian, and his ass was still lying there asleep. "Now how in the hell is his yellow ass still out of it?" I said to myself.

I walked away from the window and approached the bed.

"Brian, get up. Your bitch outside," I said, shaking him awake.

I watched him hop up and throw on his clothes like Speedy Gonzales. As he scooted past the window, trying not to be seen, I thought, *This is just too much. I don't have time for their drama.*

Ready for whatever, I put on my shorts and some shoes. I walked downstairs and opened the front door. As I looked outside, I noticed Kandy pulling off. I woke my cousin up and told her to throw on some shoes. The only thing I had on my mind was revenge.

This wench done came to my house for the last time.

I looked down and noticed this ho had stolen my damn newspaper.

"This petty bitch," I fumed.

Brian finally came downstairs to grab his truck keys. He tried to kiss my cheek, but I turned my head.

"You better check your ho and tell her to keep her ass away from my house because two can play that game," I told Brian, meaning every single word.

"I'll call you later," he replied, clearly frustrated.

"Don't bother," I said.

He stared at me, giving me the "don't play with me look". Little did he know, I was not afraid of that shit.

It was nine o'clock the next night, and I was sitting at home smoking with my two cousins, telling them about the high-speed chase when I said, "Let's go."

"Where we going?" they asked.

"That wench wanted to come to my house, so I'm about to pay her a little visit," I smirked.

Without hesitation, we all jumped into the car and took off. I knew where Kandy lived because I was with Sabrina one day when she had to stop over there for something. Even though I sat in the car, I made sure I remembered the street name, the house number, and the color of the house.

When I pulled up in front of the house, we all got out and ran up to her door. I turned around with my back facing the door and started kicking it.

"Bitch, bring yo' ass outside!" I screamed through the door.

I looked through the window and could see Brian sitting on the couch like nothing was going on.

"Brian, I'm gone kick yo' ass, too. Got this ho coming to my house for you, and you in there sitting comfortable, huh?"

I started kicking on the door again while my cousins started pounding on the door with their fists.

"Get away from my house; I'm calling the police," Kandy yelled from inside the house.

"I don't care, bitch. Answer this door," I screamed.

About ten minutes in, I started hearing police sirens in the distance.

"Come on, y'all. Fuck this ho *and* that nigga," I told them.

Before running back to the car, we kicked the door one last time. Then we jumped into the car and drove back to my place, where I ended the night hanging up on Brian when he called.

♥

I could not believe I was in a love triangle, not just with Brian and Kandy's toxic asses. I also had drama with Chucky Jr. Ever since I told him I did not want to get back with him, he had become excessively aggressive. He had been calling me out my name, starting arguments, and even putting his hands on me. Finding out Brian and I were talking made him even more furious. It was as if the news made him insane. I do not think it was because I was seeing someone else, though. I think it was because I was seeing Brian.

It was just me and Charity at home one night, basically just me because Charity was an infant. My cousins had gone to their mom's house for a few hours, and they had not made it back home yet.

I glanced at the clock, and it read 8:00 p.m. I was lying on the couch when I heard a knock on the door. With my mommy instincts kicking in, I looked over at my daughter in her swing, and then I sat up. Seconds later, I heard the knock again, so I got up and strolled to the door. I looked out the peephole but could see nothing out of it because it was dark and the light in front of the door was not coming on.

"Who is it?" I asked through the door.

"It's Chucky," I heard the voice on the other side of the door say.

I opened the storm door but not the screen door. I looked Chucky Jr. in his face while he was standing there in his blue jeans, a blue and red plaid Tommy Hilfiger button-up shirt, and some Tommy Hilfiger shoes. *His outfit is so typical*, I thought to myself.

Wondering what the hell he wanted, I stood there in a long t-shirt and some boy shorts. I had a ponytail in my hair and no shoes on.

"What you want?" I asked him through the screen.

"Is it okay if I come inside to see my daughter?" he asked.

As I looked at him, everything inside of me was telling me to say no because it was late. But I did not want any problems, so I relented.

"I guess so, but you can't stay long because it's already getting late and from now on, I would appreciate it if you would call before you come, and if you would come at a decent hour."

Reluctantly, I opened the screen door and stepped to the side so that he could come in. He stopped at

Charity's swing and picked her up. He took her into his arms and sat on the couch with her.

I walked out of the room to give them some privacy and settled in at the dining room table. I did not want to be around him because he made me feel uncomfortable.

The TV played softly in the background, so I could hear him talking and playing with Charity. Out of nowhere, it was as if Chucky Jr. had snapped because I heard him talking about me.

"Yeah, your momma don't want me no more because she has a new boyfriend."

My stomach instantly dropped because I knew it was about to be some shit. "I should have followed my first mind," I told myself.

"Guess what, Charity? Your momma is a ho." I could still hear him talking shit.

I got up from the kitchen table and walked into the living room. I stood in front of them with my hand on my hip.

"It's time for you to go," I told him, pissed off. "Go ahead and say goodbye to your daughter and raise on up out of my house."

He looked up at me and stood up, still holding Charity in his hands. He was ignoring me, continuing to talk shit about me to my daughter.

"So, your momma can have niggas in her house, but she wants to put me out," he said looking at our daughter. "Yo' momma ain't shit."

"I asked you nicely to leave. You're not about to be in my house, holding my baby while talking shit about me." I could feel the anger pumping through my body. "Get the fuck out my house!"

"I'm not going nowhere," he yelled.

Trying not to give in to Chucky Jr.'s antics, I gave myself a pep talk. *I knew this was going to be a bad idea. I just need to get out of this house and make it to the neighbor's house.*

Quickly, I walked out of the living room and headed through the kitchen to the staircase that led upstairs to the second floor. Once I made it halfway up the stairs, I felt something grab my shirt from behind. A forceful tug followed shortly after.

I fell and rolled down the stairs. While lying at the bottom of the stairs, I looked up at Chucky Jr. and noticed he was still holding my daughter in his hands. I got up and tried to run past him, but he cut me off by the kitchen sink. Now that he had me blocked in a corner, I realized I could not fight back because this idiot had my child in his arms. I could not risk her getting hurt.

"Please, just leave my house. I don't want any problems. Just leave," I cried out to him.

He refused to hear my cries and pleas. The look in his eyes told me he wanted to knock me out, and I was not going to let that happen to me, and definitely not in front of my child.

Keren, you have to get out of here, I told myself.

I looked Chucky Jr. in the eyes and said slowly but firmly, "Get the fuck . . . out of my house."

Chucky Jr. looked at me like I had said something wrong. His eyes bulged slightly, and he bit his bottom lip. Before I could say anything else, Chucky head butted me. I dropped to the ground and held my head. When he started kicking me, all I could do was ball up into the fetal position to protect my stomach and face.

The pain that shot through my body was the worst pain I had ever felt in my life. I could not believe the man I had once loved was beating on me like I was a nigga on the street. Well, I should say a female on the street because I had never seen or heard of him fighting a man before. He was probably afraid to fight another man, anyway.

As I watched the horrible scene playing out in front of me, the way Chucky Jr. was standing over me and kicking me made me question if he had ever loved me. How could you do this to the mother of your child while holding your child? *Nigga, you a bitch*, I thought constantly, but I dared not say that to him. I kept the thoughts to myself because I just wanted him to stop kicking me and to leave my house.

When I finally opened my eyes, I did not see Chucky. I slowly got up and limped into the living room, holding my left side. He had put my daughter on the couch, and he was walking out the door, shutting it behind him. I picked my baby up and rushed to the door to run next door to my friend's house. As soon as I opened the door, Chucky turned to walk back toward my door. I quickly slammed the door and locked it. I could hear him beating on the door seconds later.

Amid the chaos, I made my baby a pallet on the couch, laid her down, and went into the kitchen to finish my blunt. I needed something to calm me down because I was so pissed and so terrified.

Out of nowhere, I heard a loud crash and glass shattering. I ran back into the living room and noticed my window had been broken out. There was glass everywhere, including on the couch where my baby was lying.

At that point, I did not care anymore. I wanted Chucky Jr. to pay because my baby was on that couch, and he could have seriously hurt her. Once I checked on Charity and put her in her swing, I went to the kitchen to smoke while I waited. I made sure I gave him enough time to leave so that I could get out of the house safely.

I waited about thirty minutes before I ran next door to call the police and Brian.

"Hello," Brian answered his phone in a confused tone, most likely because he did not recognize the number.

"Hey, can you come over? Chucky just left here, and I'm scared to stay here alone."

"What you mean you're scared? What's wrong? What happened?" he asked.

"He came over here and started talking a lot of shit, mad about you. He pulled me downstairs, head-butted me, and kicked me all in my back and side while I was on the ground," I explained through my tears.

"Stop crying," he consoled me. "I'm on my way. Where you at?"

"I'm next door at the neighbor's house." I sniffled. "Oh yeah, he threw a brick through my window and shattered it."

Silence came over the phone. It worried me because I did not know what Brian was thinking.

"You there?" I asked.

"Yeah, I'm here. Stay where you at. I'm on my way."

I sat at my friend's house for twenty minutes before Brian came over. I left my daughter with my friend while I went outside to greet him.

"Get in the car," he said.

I did not know where we were going, but I figured we were going to Chucky Jr.'s house from the frown plastered on Brian's face.

He spoke only four words during our ride: "Where does he live?"

Almost robotically, I gave him the address, and I just sat there in disbelief about what had happened not even an hour before.

I was so pissed at myself for going against my better judgment and allowing him into my house, knowing I was alone and he had issues. I kept my face turned toward the passenger window because the tears were rolling down my face like a water fountain, and I did not want Brian to see me so vulnerable.

About fifteen minutes later, I looked up and noticed we were sitting in front of Chucky Jr.'s house.

"Go knock on the door," Brian told me as he climbed out of his vehicle.

Wondering what I had gotten myself into, I stepped out of the car, nervous as hell. I did not know how Chucky Jr. was going to react or how Brian was going to handle the situation. I hurried up the five stairs that led to the porch and knocked on the door and rang the doorbell.

The door opened just as I turned around to walk back off the porch. I turned back around, and I could see Chucky Jr. and his momma standing at the door. As soon as I looked at him, all my emotions poured out, and I went completely off, yelling and screaming at Chucky Jr. I called him everything but a child of God. I was walking toward the stairs to get closer to where Brian was standing near the vehicle when Chucky Jr.'s eyes grew wide.

"You brought this nigga to my house!" I heard him yell out.

"Yeah, nigga, I'm here. Come on and walk off that porch," Brian yelled back at him. "You not so tough now, are you? You jumped on her, right? Bring yo' ass off that porch, nigga."

"I'm calling the police," Chucky Jr.'s momma said, her voice frantic.

"Go ahead. Tell them how your son was just beating on me and threw a brick through my window while you're at it," I screamed at her.

I looked over at Brian walking toward the porch, but I stopped him because I did not want him to get in any trouble over me. When he looked at me, his eyes softened.

"Nigga, I'm going to see you," Brian said as he started walking back toward the sidewalk where the car was parked.

"Let's go," he said to me.

We got into the car and pulled off. During the ride back to my house, Brian just kept mumbling under his breath that he was going to get that scary ass nigga, and he could not believe they wanted to call the police.

"I will be back; give me twenty minutes," he said once he dropped me off.

I walked next door to get my baby and then walked back home. I locked all the doors and put something up to my window to cover the hole, at least until the apartment office sent someone over to fix it.

Still in disbelief, I sat on the couch with my blunt, reflecting on all the drama I had endured that day. I could not believe my life had come to this. I could not believe God was allowing me to go through so much shit. What had I done that was so bad to receive this type of punishment? This was no kind of life to be living. It was pure hell, and I could not live like this anymore. If this was what my life was going to be, I did not want to live it. I did not want to endure this pain any longer.

I thought my days of having my heart and mind filled with so much negativity were over, but on that day, they seemed to be far from over. However, I knew I had to stay strong and live for my child. I just prayed that God would give me the strength I needed to continue living.

♥

The situationship between me and Brian continued on for another few months, three to be exact. That's when I found out I was pregnant. I had been feeling sick and unable to keep anything down, so the first thing I did was take a pregnancy test. Because I recognized the symptoms from my first experience, I knew something was not right.

I peed on the stick and waited two minutes for the results. As I waited, millions of thoughts circled around my head. I did not know what I was going to do if the test came back positive. How was I going to support another child when my daughter had just turned one? How in the hell did I allow my ass to get knocked up by a man I was not even with? I was so scared. My stomach was turning in so many knots, and it seemed like I had to poop, but I knew it was just my nerves. I went through the process alone because I did not want anyone to judge me, and because I believed I *had* to do it alone.

That was the longest two minutes in history. Each minute felt like an hour. I picked up the stick and instantly knew what the plus sign meant. I WAS FUCKING PREGNANT! And I was pregnant by a man whom I wanted nothing else to do with. A man whom I knew I would not be with. A man who was great at playing games and was only serious about his money. I smelled trouble already. *Is that something I want to deal with?* I wondered.

I was not too fond of the decision I made, but I thought it was the best decision for me. I weighed the pros and cons, and I even prayed about it. After a few weeks, I was finally at a point where I was going to be okay with my choice. I was going to abort the pregnancy. Now, I just needed to tell Brian.

Because I preferred not to tell him about the pregnancy over the phone, and I wanted to make sure I had all my words thought out and put together, I did not tell Brian right away. It had been a week since I found out about the pregnancy when I finally broke the news to Brian that he would be a father again, and I did not plan on keeping it.

I was sitting on my mother's porch watching the neighborhood kids play outside that day. It was around midday, and the sun was beaming. A neighbor was washing his car, and another neighbor was on the porch braiding a guy's hair. I was puffing on my blunt and enjoying the scenery, trying to get up the nerve to dial the seven digits that would jingle Brian's phone.

"What's up?" Brian answered, sounding as if he was in the middle of something.

"Hey, what you doing?" I asked him, not really caring but trying to make small talk before I hit him with the news.

"Handling some business. What's up?" he asked again.

"I didn't want to have this conversation over the phone, but I just wanted to tell you I'm pregnant," I blurted out.

There was a short, awkward pause between us. I sat there wondering what the hell he was thinking as I puffed on my blunt.

"Are you sure?" he asked, the concern heightened in his voice.

"Yes, I am sure. I took the dang test twice and both times positive." I rolled my eyes as I responded to his dumb question.

I was going to let him sit there and squirm on the other side of the phone, but I did not feel like answering any more questions. His tone told me everything I needed to know.

Before he could say another word, I said, "Don't worry. I don't want to keep it."

"Are you serious?" he asked, not out of concern for me aborting his child, but out of the excitement of me not wanting to keep it. Saying that his response pissed me off would have been an understatement.

"I called a place in St. Louis, and they do it, but I will have to go next week, or it will be too late. So I need you to take me there," I told him, clearly annoyed.

"That's cool. I can take you," he said.

I bet you could.

"I will call you after I set up the appointment so you'll know what time I need to be there," I said abruptly, trying to end the conversation.

"Okay," was all he said before hanging up.

I took the last pull off my blunt and blew the smoke out, hoping to blow all the other bullshit out of my mind right along with it.

The ride to St. Louis was so uncomfortable. I sat in the passenger seat as quiet as a church mouse. While my mouth could not form any words, my brain was on full blast. My number one concern was, *Am I doing the right thing*? The closer we got to St. Louis, the more I wondered if I should change my mind. I was so confused and scared.

From start to finish, the entire process took about four hours. After I signed in, they called me to the back, where they took a sonogram to see how far along I was. They drew some blood and then I had to go through a counseling session to make sure I was not being forced to terminate the pregnancy. I was so scared because this was all new to me, and I kept asking myself if I was sure.

The procedure itself took about fifteen minutes. I lay there with my legs open and the doctor between them, using some type of vacuum-like tool to remove my baby, as tears poured down my face. This was my baby I was killing, and it was killing me to the core.

The two-and-a-half-hour ride home was again quiet, and the tension was as thick as fog in the early morning. I sat there with my arms folded and my head facing the grass lining the road. I cried so much that my eyes turned red and puffy, and so much regret filled me on the inside. What hurt the most was that Brian never tried to console me or even ask if I was okay. I knew for a fact I would no longer deal with him. I knew this was the end of the road for us.

I thought the chapter between Brian and me was closed until Sabrina came over a few weeks later, telling me Kandy had died and Brian was being held accountable for it.

The bomb Sabrina had dropped on me turned my world upside down. I could not believe how close to home that was. So many times, I thought about how that could have been me. I would be lying if I said hearing this devastating news did not make me feel better about ending my pregnancy.

Kandy's death affected my life so badly that I could not trust any man for a while, including my dad and my brother. I often wondered, how was I to get over this trauma? How was I to get over anything that had happened in my life?

Chapter 14

Still reeling from the possibility of Brian being connected to Kandy's tragic death, I tried to reevaluate my life. I moved back home with my mom and siblings because I could not take being out on my own. The thought terrified me, and my anxiety ran high. I also needed help raising Charity because I was suffering mentally. I was in no shape to do it alone.

During that time, I started hanging out with Tish and Sharen, a couple of girls I knew from school. Sharen lived around the corner from my mom's house, and we even registered for classes together at the local college. As she and I became closer, we would ride to class together, and when we were not in school, we would ride around smoking and drinking.

Sharen was dating a guy who lived in Chicago, and Tish and I would entertain his two friends. Everything was cool until Sharen began traveling to Chicago to visit her boo. I had nothing else to do, so I would jump at the chance to spend time with my girls. This feeling did not last long because my ancestors woke my ass up and told me I was moving way too fast and doing way too much.

The last three times we drove to Chicago, we experienced some bizarre things. The first thing was the headlights going out on our way back to Peoria. We had to drive all the way home with no headlights. While everyone else might have ignored it, I thought of it as a sign. The second time, I was driving but was about to miss the exit. We did a 360 in the middle of the highway and drove off the road into a ditch. We stood on the side of the highway at night with our thumbs in the air like some hitchhikers. Thankfully, a young white guy pulled over and backed us out of the field. Even though we could drive the rest of the way home with no problem, I believed that incident was another sign.

Now the third time was much more serious and life-threatening. I was sitting on my mom's porch one evening, smoking a blunt, when I spotted Sharen pulling up in a silver Chrysler that her brother had rented for her. I noticed Tish sitting on the passenger side.

"Hey, girl. What you up to?" Sharen asked.

"Not much . . . sitting here bored as hell. What y'all up to?" I responded after blowing a cloud of smoke.

Sharen and Tish got out of the car, bringing with them a half-pint of Remy VSOP, and sat on the porch with me.

"You know my birthday's coming up, and I wanted to go to Chicago to spend the weekend with my boo. You want to roll?" Sharen asked me.

I stopped in the middle of my pull and looked from her to Tish, wondering what the hell they were up to.

"I don't know. The last two times we went up there, we had some kind of incident go down with us," I said skeptically.

I looked at Tish again. "Girl, you going, too?"

Tish took a sip of the Remy and said, "Yeah, I guess so. I don't have anything else planned."

"I'm down this last time if I get a babysitter," I told them. Then I paused. "Hold on. Where the hell are we staying?" I asked, confused.

"At his sister's house . . . she said we are welcome to stay there," she replied.

I gave her my famous who-pooted face and took a long, hard pull off my blunt. Though I was going along with the plan, thoughts of doubt circled around my mind.

The following weekend, we drove two and a half hours to Chicago. I drove with Sharen sitting in the passenger seat and Tish sitting in the back. I drove eighty to eighty-five miles per hour the whole way, listening to DTP. "RPM" by Shawnna was one of my favorite songs from their album.

We arrived in Chicago at 6:30 that evening. As soon as we got there, I pulled into the gas station because I had to use the bathroom and Sharen had to call her dude to let him know we were there. We also needed him to give us directions to our destination.

Once we reached the spot, Tim, Sharen's friend, and his friend, Lonnie, met us outside. Lonnie was the friend who liked me. Even though we had been communicating, it was nothing serious and definitely nothing to write home about.

Tim had a dark brown complexion, a short haircut, and a slim, medium build. He walked out of the house wearing some black jeans, a red and black hoodie, and some black boots. In contrast, Lonnie was a light-skinned guy with a short haircut and full lips. He was wearing a gray and white sweatsuit and some white gym shoes. He was not my cup of tea at all, but I entertained him because I was running an interference for my homegirl.

As Tim took over as the driver, I got in the backseat along with Tish. Lonnie crawled into the backseat, too, leaving me in the middle.

"Where you girls trying to go?" Tim asked us.

"This your city," Tish and I said simultaneously.

I continued with, "I know I need to get me some weed, though."

The sun had already set, and nightfall was creeping upon us. As we were riding, all the people I saw outside took me aback. People were hanging on the corners, standing in front of the stores, and sitting outside on cars and on porches.

I could not explain the feeling I had, but I knew something was not right. It was as if I knew everything would not go as planned that weekend and that we might have been in over our heads. It seemed as if danger was lurking.

We pulled up in front of some projects about fifteen minutes later. After Tim put the car in park, he announced, "This is where the weed is. Y'all come on, and I will introduce y'all."

"Trina, this is my girl, Sharen, and these are her friends, Tish and Keren," Tim said once we stepped out of the car. "They want to buy some weed."

Trina was not a big girl, but she was on the thicker side. She wore blue jeans, a white tee, and some Jordans. She had cornrows in her hair, two gold chains around her neck, and a gold ring on each finger. Simply put, Trina looked like she was "'bout that life".

"Hello," we all said in unison.

"What are you looking for?" Trina asked us.

"I just want a dub," I responded, asking for twenty dollars' worth of weed.

Trina reached into this purple Crown Royal bag and pulled out a couple of pre-made bags of weed, and then she told us to pick the one we wanted. I quickly grabbed a bag and got back into the car. I started rolling up to ease the uneasy feeling roaring in the pit of my stomach.

Shortly after, Tim pulled up to a spot across the street from the projects. He turned the music up and got out of the car. As he stood outside talking to some guys, I sat there wondering what they were talking about and when we were going to the club.

Ten minutes later, Tim climbed back into the car and pulled off from the parking lot. He pulled back around to the projects and hopped out of the car. As soon as he got out, a car pulled up on the side of the car we were sitting in. A guy jumped out of the driver's seat and another one out the back on the driver's side, both of them wielding two big guns.

"Duck," I yelled out as I watched the two guys take aim at Tim.

A spray of bullets followed Tim as he took off, running past the car. Seconds later, the shooters jumped back into their car and pulled off. One of the bullets had entered through the front windshield of our car and exited out the back window right beside Tish's head. Thankfully, the bullet had missed her.

I climbed over the seat and jumped into the driver's seat to pull off.

"What are you doing?" Sharen yelled at me.

"I'm leaving," I yelled back, slightly pissed she had even asked me that.

"No, we can't leave Tim out there," she responded in fear.

"Fuck that! We need to get out of here," Tish shouted at Sharen.

"We are not leaving him," Sharen insisted.

Tish and I looked at each other, pissed off that she was worried about this nigga when he had put us in harm's way. Our lives could have easily ended because of what had just happened, and she was not taking it seriously.

Shortly after, Tim came running from in between the buildings and yanked the car door open. I climbed back into the back seat, and he sped off like a bat out of hell.

I sat in the back seat, scared as hell and ready to go home. My heart was beating fast, and my hands were shaking. A steady stream of tears rolled down my face. My anxiety had reached its peak.

"What am I going to do? I can't go back home with this hole in the windshield like this. My brother's going to kill me," Sharen said in a panic.

"I got a guy who can take care of that before you guys leave," Tim said nonchalantly.

"I'm ready to go home. It's not safe being here with him," I interjected.

"I'm ready to go, too," Tish added.

"Can we please stay the night, y'all? I really need to get this window fixed," Sharen pleaded, looking back at us.

I noticed Tim speeding down streets and alleyways. While I did not know where he was going, I quietly prayed that God would grant us mercy and that we would make it out of Chicago alive.

As Tim continued driving, I gazed out the window, still in disbelief. He drove for another twenty minutes before we pulled into someone's garage.

"Come on," Tim said as he climbed out of the car.

We all sat there and just stared at each other.

"It's okay. You'll be safe here. This is my sister's house," he assured us.

The girls and I exchanged glances, and then we grabbed our bags and climbed out of the car. We followed Tim into the house and down some stairs to a basement. I did not understand why we were going over there; I just wanted to hit the highway and go home.

The basement was set up with a living room and a bedroom off to the side. I guess the bedroom was Tim's room because he walked in and shut the door.

"We're leaving tomorrow with or without that window fixed," Tish told Sharen. She and I both had had enough.

Without saying a word, Sharen got up and went into the bedroom with Tim. I lay down on the couch where I was sitting, and Tish climbed on the other couch and pulled her coat up over her. I struggled to fall asleep because I had so much on my mind.

I can't believe I could've lost my life tonight, I thought. *Death was staring us all in the face, and here we are still in this death-ass city.*

This was the third and last time. I knew something was going to happen, but I went against my intuition, and it almost cost me everything. I had a little girl I needed to take care of, and I could not do that if I were dead.

Yes, the ancestors were watching out for me, but they also tried to warn me. My stubborn, hard-headed ass still did not listen. Yet, I heard them loud and clear as I lay there on the couch: my days of visiting Chicago were over. I realized I loved my life, and I wanted to live.

The next morning came, and Tim's guy said he could not fix the car window until Monday. We refused to stay until then, so we had no choice but to put some tape over the windshield hole and head back home.

GOODBYE, CHICAGO! I screamed on the inside. I was so thankful to leave, and I knew I would never have to look back.

♥

After realizing I was moving too fast in the streets, I knew I needed to slow my ass down and take it easy on the ride of life. I would still hang out with my friends, but I left all the Chicago trips to them. I had had my fair share, not to mention I was terrified of that place.

During that time, I reconnected with an old friend, Craig. He was one of the guys I used to talk to from the south end of town. We had met a few years before, and it did not go much further than talking on the phone. I figured he did not want to go further back then because I was younger than him and still under my stepdad's thumb.

The first time I met Craig, I spotted him at a party. A girl I knew from the block I lived on introduced me to him. The next time I ran into him, I saw him at the liquor store, and he instantly knew who I was.

Craig was light-skinned with a medium height and build, and he rocked a short haircut and a gold tooth. Craig was so fine to me; he was handsome with mad swag. On the day he walked up to me at Sheridan Liquors, he sported some blue jeans, a white tee, some white and blue Nikes, and a gold chain. I was standing in the line, waiting to approach the counter, as he walked up, and I caught him staring at me. I glanced at him, and he smiled big, showing off his gold tooth.

"How you been doing, sweetie?" Craig said.

"I've been good. Thanks for asking. And how about you?" I asked.

"I've been good, living," he responded.

"That's what's up," I said to him, smiling hard, trying not to make it obvious that my eyes were scanning his body up and down.

"Well, we should catch up. Can I get your number?" he asked.

"Only if you're going to use it," I responded flirtatiously.

Craig took out his phone and saved my number in it. The whole time I could not stop smiling at him.

He still looks so damn good, I thought to myself. Even as we still stood in line, I could not wait for him to call me.

"I'll hit you up later, okay?"

"That's fine. I'll be waiting."

That encounter was the start of a special bond. Whenever you saw Craig, you saw me. He had become one of my best friends, as well as the man I was dating.

I could tell Craig anything, and he would not judge me. He also got along well with my homegirls, and we all would kick it together on the regular.

One Saturday night, I told Craig I wanted some pancakes, so we headed down University Street to Perkins Restaurant. I was driving Craig's cousin's car because Craig did not have a license. Shortly after, I motioned to turn left on War Memorial, and the police turned on their sirens and lights behind me. I made the turn and pulled over because I knew I was the one they wanted.

A black police officer walked up to the driver's side window. He had a bald head and wore glasses. I glanced at his badge and noticed it read "Allen".

I recognized the officer instantly. He used to be a teacher at my high school.

"Can you roll the window down, please?" Officer Allen said.

I complied and rolled the window down.

"Do you know why I pulled you over?" he asked.

"No, I'm sorry, but I have no idea," I responded.

"The reason I pulled you over was because you cut me off. You cut in front of me and didn't use your signal," he explained.

I thought to myself, *This fucker is lying*. I knew I did not cut him off because I saw him and used my signal.

"I need your license and insurance," he demanded.

I looked in my purse for my license, and Craig searched the glove compartment box for the insurance card. After a few seconds, I handed Officer Allen my license, but Craig could not seem to find the insurance card.

"Hold tight while I run your information," he said. "I also need you to step outside the car."

"What did I do?" I asked him.

"This car smells like marijuana, and I need you to step out of the car," he ordered.

As I opened the door to climb out of the car, another squad car pulled up.

I knew I had nothing illegal on me, so I was not worried about that part; I was nervous because I did not know what they would find on Craig.

Even though both officers searched the vehicle and found nothing, they still hauled me off to jail because of my suspended license. I did not know my license was suspended, but apparently, I was supposed to take a class when I got the transportation of alcohol charge with Chucky Jr.'s brother. Because I never took the class, they had suspended my license.

I stood there, my heart pounding and stomach cramping because I was so nervous. This was the first time I had been arrested. I did not know what to expect, and I was terrified to say the least.

Officer Allen had put me in handcuffs and sat me in the back seat of his car. I did not know what they were saying to Craig, but he looked pissed. It seemed as if Craig was arguing with the officers.

"Oh my gosh, just please be quiet before both of our asses end up going to jail," I blurted out, but only loud enough for me to hear.

Ten minutes later, the wagon pulled up to transport me to the county jail. They put me on the women's side of the wagon. I was the only one on the women's side, but by the voices I heard, I could tell the men's side was full.

It took about fifteen minutes to get to the county jail. We then had to wait about thirty minutes for the personnel to process us before I was free to go. Craig had already made it there and paid for my bond.

My first experience in lockup was not as bad as I thought it would be; I was not there long enough to find out more. However, it would not be my last time going.

Craig and I dated for about six months before he broke up with me because of a misunderstanding. Or maybe it was just an excuse to leave me alone. He swore up and down that he saw a guy run out my mom's back door when he pulled up to our house, and he swore the guy was for me. I tried to explain that he was not there for me, and that it was one of my brother's friends, but he still did not believe a word I said.

I was so hurt because I really liked Craig, and I was telling the truth. Even though I did not want us to end, I was not about to chase him or spend my precious time convincing him I was telling the truth. I often told myself, *If he cared, he would have believed me.*

Unfortunately, that was the end of us, but I knew it was really over when I went to the liquor store with my homegirls and saw Craig with another girl. I could not believe my eyes.

What the fuck? I thought to myself. *It hasn't even been two days yet. Typical nigga . . . fuck him.*

I got my bottle of Remy and two Swishers, ready to drink and smoke the pain away.

"Girl, I can't believe his ass," my homegirls said in sync, like they had rehearsed the line.

I did not care, though. I was on the road to forgetting about Craig, but I had to take a detour first.

Chapter 15

Usually, I did not go for the all-out bad boy type, but there was something different about David. He was a short, thin, dark-skinned guy who wore braids and had two gold teeth in his mouth. If you would have seen how David looked back then, he would have reminded you of the rapper Meek Mill.

I met David through my girl Sharen. She was messing with David's friend, and they all were standing outside Sharen's house one day. David did not say much to me that day, but later on, I found out he had told Sharen to hook him up with me.

David and I started off talking on the phone, but then things moved pretty quickly between us. I began spending most of my time at David's house. I would call for David to pick me up or ask Sharen to drop me off at his house, with Charity in tow, of course.

While I hate to admit it, I clung to David. I craved his time and attention. But the more time I spent with him, the more I realized he was all bad for me.

The worst part? I learned David was involved with other females and not just one or two; he was involved with multiple women.

On top of other girls, David also had beef in the streets and was always in some mess.

I glanced at the clock one night and noticed the time was ten o'clock. I had just put Charity to bed and was bored out of my mind, so I called David to see what he had going on.

"Hello," he answered. I could hear laughter in the background.

"What you doing?" I asked him.

"Not much. What's up?" he responded, while talking to the people in his background.

"I'm bored. Come get me," I told him. He already knew what time it was because I called him with the same line most nights.

"Alright, I will be there in a minute," he replied.

"Okay," I said before hanging up the phone.

About thirty minutes later, David pulled up in front of my house with his friend Tone driving the car.

"What's up y'all?" I said as I hopped into the backseat of the car.

"What's going on?" Tone said.

David turned to face me and handed me a bottle of Remy and a blunt. "You looking good," he said.

I had left the house wearing a white t-shirt and some black sweat shorts and flip-flops with my hair pulled back in a low ponytail.

"I know," I said, giving him my flirty laugh.

David smiled and opened his mouth to speak, but an incoming call broke his focus.

"Hello," he said, answering his cell phone.

I did not know who he was talking to or what they were saying to him, but whatever they said had pissed him off. I noticed a scowl covering his face and anger filling his voice as he said, "I'm on my way."

David hung up the phone and started conversing with Tone, but I could not hear what they were saying because they were bumping Bone Crusher's "Never Scared" on the car stereo.

Ten minutes later, we pulled up in front of the Equator Club, and their friend Larry climbed into the backseat with me.

I looked over at Larry and instantly thought, *Damn!* Whoever he was fighting had done a number on his face. Quickly, I turned my head because I did not want him to think I was staring at him, even though I was.

David turned toward the backseat and handed Larry a gun. Immediately, I became nervous because I was still unaware of what was going on, and just the sight of guns made me uncomfortable.

Larry was so pissed. He kept moving, yelling, and spitting as he was telling Tone and David what had happened, which added to my anxiety.

"We gone find these niggas," David snarled.

Oh shit, I thought.

We rode around for about two hours, looking for whoever had jumped Larry. It seemed as if we had hit every block, street, club, alleyway, and store in the town, and honestly, I just wanted to go home. I did not want to be caught in the middle of a shootout or the police pulling us over. But I just sat in the backseat terrified, too afraid to tell David to take me home.

Suddenly, we came to a stop in front of an apartment building. Tone and Larry climbed out of the car, but David stopped to turn and look at me. He handed me the gun and said, "When you see that truck ride by, shoot."

I took the gun but shot David a look of disgust as I grasped it. Nervous as hell, I prayed the truck would not drive past us. I knew I wouldn't pull the trigger. I just couldn't.

Lord, please get me out of this. I just want to go home, I thought to myself.

Once fifteen minutes had passed, I was no longer frightened. I was pissed because I could not believe David had left me in the car for that long. I was ready to shoot his ass now.

As soon as the three of them got back into the car, I immediately said, "Take me home!"

"What's wrong with you?" David asked in a confused voice.

"I just want to go home, and I would appreciate it if you would take me home now, please," I demanded. David looked at me with a mixture of confusion and irritation on his face, but he gave Tone the sign to go ahead.

That's what I thought. I rolled my eyes and gazed out the window, too furious to look in David's direction.

When Tone pulled up to my house, I jumped out of the car and ran up to the porch, marching straight into the house. I do not remember shutting the door, and I know I did not say bye. I was so thankful the Lord had allowed me to make it home safely, but I was through with David's ass . . . for the moment.

Three days passed without me going over to David's house or even calling him. Although it was hard because I had grown accustomed to being around him every day, I knew I had to keep my distance because I did not want to be an innocent bystander caught up in somebody else's drama.

On the fourth day, I was sitting on the porch around 5:30 that Friday evening, watching my brother Bobby and his friends standing around in the yard talking and laughing. Our neighbor, Ms. Shelly, was out there on the grill cooking, and the lesbian couple across the street was on their porch, drinking and playing their music. It felt like the perfect Friday.

I sat there enjoying the scenery when my phone rang. I opened my phone and saw it was David and rolled my eyes.

As I set the phone on the porch, ignoring the call, the phone rang again.

"Yeah," I answered.

"What you mean 'yeah,'" David responded.

"What's up, David?" I asked him with some attitude in my voice.

"What you doing?" he asked.

"Sitting here on the porch. Why? What's up?" I asked, my attitude fading a bit.

"I want to see you," he said.

"So," I said, trying to act hard.

"Quit playing with me, Keren. You heard what I said."

"I hear you."

"Well, call me when you ready."

"Yep," I told him before I hung up the phone.

I would have never told him, but I did kind of miss him even though I knew he was no good for me. All I could hear was my intuition screaming, *Run, girl, because this nigga gone hurt you!* But I thought I was grown, so I just ignored it.

Lost in my thoughts, I sat on the porch for another twenty minutes before I got up and hopped into the shower. I threw on a pair of blue jean shorts, a pink and lime green shirt, and some pink flip-flops. I combed my hair down and put on a headband to keep my hair from flying in my face.

"Mom, can I use your car for an hour or two?" I asked my mother as she was sitting at the dining room table, talking on the phone.

"Why? Where are you going?" she asked me.

"Just over to hang with Sharen and Tish for a while."

"Keren, don't be drinking or smoking in my car. That's a new car, and you are not on my insurance," she said, the irritation in her voice quite obvious.

"I'm not. I promise," I pleaded with her.

Not giving my mom much time to change her mind, I grabbed the keys and hurried out the door. I drove around the corner to pick up Sharen and Tish. Then we went to buy water guns from the dollar store before driving back to Sharen's house to fill them up.

Thirty minutes later, we pulled up in David's driveway and put the car in park.

"Come here, David," I called out to him.

I sat there in the driver's seat as I watched him get off the porch and walk toward the car. As soon as he bent over the window, we fired our water guns at him, soaking him. We also started squirting the guns toward the truck before we backed up and pulled off.

We drove around a couple of blocks before passing by David's house again. We were cruising by when we heard something hit the car. I pulled up the street and got out to investigate the noise. Can you believe that bastard had the nerve to throw an egg at my mom's car?

Springing into action, I pulled into the liquor store parking lot and walked into the store to buy two cartons of eggs. We pulled back around to David's house, and as I drove by, Sharen and Tish threw the eggs toward David's house. That was the start of a major egg fight.

The egg fight lasted for a couple of hours, starting at David's house and traveling to the liquor store and to the blocks behind his house. There were at least ten to fifteen of us out there throwing eggs. It was fun until someone called the police and we had to cancel the fight.

I know this might sound strange, but that was one thing I liked about David. He was fun to be with. He could always make me smile.

Even though he knew how to make me smile, David also knew how to make me cry. After every high period, I would hit a low one. That is exactly how I felt knowing he was entertaining other females. I knew I had to leave him alone because I could not handle the way he played with my emotions. I could not handle having a repeat of the past.

The tip of the iceberg happened one Thursday summer morning. I had plans to go over to David's house to braid his hair, but I did not want to take Charity with me because his house was no place for kids.

"What are you guys going to do this morning?" I asked my parents.

"We are about to go to breakfast, and then we have some errands to run," my mom replied. "Why?"

"I was going to see if you guys could keep Charity for a couple hours so I can go and braid David's hair. I don't want to take her because I believe the police are going to raid his spot," I told them.

"We are not going to be able to do that today," Bobby said.

"Okay, well, can you guys drop us off over there then?" I asked them, hoping to compromise.

Once they agreed, my mom and stepdad drove the six-minute trip from our house to David's house to drop me and Charity off. While I thought they would have questioned me along the way, the ride was mostly quiet.

"We will call you when we get done to see where you guys are at and if you need a ride back home," my stepdad said.

"Okay," I said, climbing out of the car with Charity on my hip.

I was at David's house long enough to roll a blunt, set Charity on the couch next to me, and grab the comb to start David's hair before we heard a knock on the back door. About a split second later, another one sounded at the front door.

David told one of his friends to answer the front door for him. Because his house saw people coming in and out all day long, he was not even paying attention to the door.

"Who is it?" the friend asked as he stood next to the door.

"Police," the voice on the other side responded.

"Who is it?" David asked, inhaling the smoke from the blunt.

"I think they said the police," the friend responded nervously.

At that moment, I looked up and noticed David had taken off running and his friend had turned to walk away from the door. Before his friend could go anywhere, the door flew open and police rushed in with their guns drawn out and yelling, "POLICE! FREEZE!"

I sat there on the couch, horrified, as I held my baby with handcuffed hands and an officer stood over me with a gun pointed at my head.

That was the most terrifying experience because I did not know what to expect. I did not know what David had in his house, and I did not know if they were going to take my baby. But I knew once I got out of this, I had to do things differently. I knew I could not continue living my life the way I was living it.

Thankfully, I walked away from that raid with no issues, and without DCFS being involved. I also walked away from David with ease, having no regrets and not caring what anyone said or thought about me. And, of course, David went to jail.

I knew I could not allow my parents to find out about the raid, but I also knew I needed to get out and clear that traumatic incident from my mind. When the weekend came, I went out with Sharen and Tish just to kick it and paid my little sister, Precious, to babysit for me. When I made it home that night, my stepdad was sitting at my mom's dining room table, talking to my mom. By this time, he had already moved out of the house.

Even though I never said anything, I felt some type of way when Bobby moved out because it seemed like he was abandoning us. It seemed as if he did not care and took the easy way out. I was unaware of what was really going on, but I knew I loved my stepdad, and I did not want him to leave us.

I shuffled through the door, high as hell and a little tipsy. I was not in the mood for anything other than eating and going to bed, but as soon as I shut the door, my parents went in on me.

"Where you been?" Bobby asked me.

"I was out with Sharen and Tish," I responded.

"Me and your mom was talking, and we feel like you spending way too much time out kicking it, and you need to get your life together," my stepdad said.

"You have a daughter that you need to be taking care of, instead of being in those streets," my mom added.

I stood there with my hands on my hips, rolling my eyes and giving off major attitude. I knew they were right, but they were blowing my high, and I just wanted them to leave me alone so that I could eat.

"You have your whole life ahead of you, and you need to focus on raising Charity," my stepdad continued.

"What? Like you? You don't care. Didn't you leave us?" I snapped, asking my own questions now. "And I helped raise y'all kids. Why can't y'all raise mine?"

"This conversation is about you and that little girl up there asleep. That's my granddaughter and not my daughter," my mom stressed.

With my high almost completely blown, I pulled out my phone and dialed Chucky Jr.'s number.

"Hello," Chucky Jr. answered, sounding like he might have been lying down.

"Hey, I need you to come and get Charity because my parents are tripping, and I'm about to leave here and don't know where I'm going," I cried out to him angrily.

"Okay, I'm on my way," he said before hanging up the phone.

It took Chucky Jr. about ten minutes to arrive at my mom's house. When I heard his truck pull up, I met him outside.

I was standing on the porch when he got out of the truck, looking both half-asleep and confused.

"What's going on?" he asked.

"I have to get out of this house tonight, and I don't know where I'm going to go, but I know I can't have my baby out here. I need you to take her for the night," I explained to him.

"Why don't we take a ride and smoke a blunt, give you the chance to calm down?" he offered.

"Okay," I agreed. Anything was better than staying there, so I climbed into his truck, and we drove off.

"I have to stop here first to get the weed," Chucky Jr. said as he pulled up to the house he lived in with his aunt.

He ran into the house and came back out about three minutes later. Then he climbed back into the car, and we pulled off.

The car ride was quiet and a little awkward because I had not really talked to Chucky Jr. since he assaulted me and threw a brick through my window. I hated having to call him, but I needed to get away.

Five minutes later, we pulled up to a cluster of apartments across the street from the Kroger grocery store.

"This my uncle Matt's house," Chucky Jr. said.

I wondered why we were there, but I did not question it.

We got out of the truck and walked up to his uncle's door. Chucky knocked on the door, and his uncle Matt opened the door seconds later. We walked in and his uncle walked back to his room, not saying a word. After we sat on the couch, Chucky turned on the TV and flipped through the stations until he stopped on *The Wayans Bros.* It was the episode where Marlon and Shawn had added some meat to their dad's pot of chili for a competition, only to find out later it was actually dog food.

While I was watching TV, Chucky Jr. was breaking down the swisher. Once he finished that task, he broke down the weed.

The energy between us was still dry, and I felt a little uneasy. I sat with my legs crossed at my ankles and my arms folded at my chest.

Chucky took his lighter and dried the blunt after rolling it, and then he handed the blunt to me.

I lit the blunt and took a nice, long pull. I exhaled and pulled off it again and then passed the blunt back to Chucky. When I turned my attention back to the TV, I began feeling weird.

Chucky Jr. passed the blunt back to me, and I hit it again, but this time I took a light pull from it because I was not feeling right.

"Here, I'm not feeling right," I told Chucky Jr. as I handed him the blunt. "I'm done with it."

Chucky Jr. said nothing. He just looked at me.

"I'm ready to go home," I told him.

Chucky looked at me with a weird look in his eyes and said, "Give me a kiss."

I gave him the who-pooted face mixed with a little confusion.

"You gone make me ask you again? Give me a kiss," he demanded.

I did not want to give him a kiss, but the aggression in his voice made me nervous, and I did not want any issues. To keep the peace, I gave him a peck on the lips.

"Now, can you please take me home?" I asked him.

He stood up and turned off the TV. Following his lead, I walked out the door and back to the truck.

I got in on the passenger side and watched him as he fumbled with something behind his seat.

"I have to keep this in here in case I'm the only one on the streets," Chucky Jr. said.

I was confused about what he was saying and why he was saying it to me. My heart was pounding wildly, and my body was sweating profusely. All I could think about was what in the hell was wrong with him, and what in the hell had this negro given me.

As we headed down the street, I noticed he was taking the long way to my mom's house, and that he kept sticking his hands in his pockets.

"What are you doing? Why do you keep putting your hands in your pockets?" I asked him as I watched him turn down my mom's street.

He answered with a question. "Why? You thought I was going to kill you?"

After hearing those words, I jumped out of the truck before it completely stopped in my mom's yard. My heart was still pounding as I ran. My mom's porch had five stairs to climb, but I believe my feet hit only one.

Panicked, I stood at the front door, trying to hurry and get my keys out of my pocket. It seemed as if I could not move fast enough, so I started banging on my mom's door.

"Who is it?" my mom asked, the irritation oozing from her voice.

"It's me," my voice cracked, full of terror.

As my mom answered the door, I looked back toward Chucky Jr.'s truck and noticed he was pulling off.

I turned back around to face my mom, and she must have seen the terror on my face.

"Girl, what's wrong with you?" she asked, worried.

Falling into my mom's arms, I blurted out, "I think Chucky put something into the blunt I smoked with him. I don't feel right at all."

"You want me to take you to the hospital?" she asked.

"No, but I need to get out of this stuff because I feel hot and my heart is beating fast," I said, hyperventilating.

My mom started walking toward the kitchen as I stood there in the dining room, stripping out of my clothes.

I did not know what was wrong with me. My mind kept wondering what the hell had Chucky given me, and what would make him ask if I thought he was going to kill me. Then my mind rushed over to Kandy and how she died mysteriously, or may have been killed. How they discovered her body in a trash bag hidden in an abandoned warehouse turned my stomach. Clearly, my mind was all over the place, and I was tripping out.

My mom ran into the room with a towel and a cup of water. I wrapped that towel around my naked body and started guzzling the water so fast.

It was about midnight when I finally settled down. I ended my night sitting on the porch, still wrapped in a towel, wondering how my life was so screwed up and thinking about how I thought Chucky Jr. tried to drug me.

I just could not understand what I had done so wrong in my life that I had to endure so much. I was beyond sick of it.

♥

Six months had passed since the raid at David's house, and I had not heard from him or anyone who associated with him until . . .

One Wednesday afternoon, I was sitting on my mother's porch, smoking a blunt and listening to R. Kelly on the radio. I was sitting there puffing and singing "You Remind Me of Something". I probably sounded like a broke dick dog as I sang along, but I was in my own world and loving every minute of it. That is when the phone interrupted my vibe.

"Hello," I answered, hoping the phone call would be quick.

"Is this Keren?" the male voice on the other end of the phone asked.

"Yes," I said, confused.

I was trying to catch the voice to see if I could make out who it was, but I had never heard it before.

"Who is this?" I asked the caller.

"This is Jim, David's cousin," the guy said.

Just like that muthafucka to ruin my day, I thought to myself.

"How can I help you?" I asked, quite annoyed.

"I'm sorry to call you, but I received a letter from David the other day from prison, and there was a letter addressed to you in the envelope. He gave me your number and asked if I would deliver it to you," Jim explained. "He also told me where you live at and wanted to know if you would meet me to get it. I only stay around the corner," he added.

Against my better judgment, I replied, "Sure."

In retrospect, I wish I would have left that letter right where it was because it was definitely one big ass lesson for me.

After replying to that first letter, I exchanged many letters with David while he was in prison. I allowed his jailhouse talk to reel me back in. I got sucked in with the "I want and need you" and "I love you" lines. The main thing was how he said he wanted to live with me and we were going to be together when he came home. And what the hell did I do?

I found my own house and moved out of my mother's house.

I got a phone turned on and the collect call block turned off so that David could call whenever he wanted.

I even allowed the negro to move in with me and get paroled to my house.

After all the efforts I made to make coming home comfortable for this scammer, I soon found out he was still a liar, a cheater, and a manipulator. Nothing had changed.

Not only was he messing with Brenda, LaTisha, Linda, and Felicia, but the asshole was also messing with someone I considered a friend. Someone who had been over to my house, slept on my couch, and eaten my food.

Now I would be lying if I said I was not hurt because I most definitely was, but I was determined to get him back and remove him from my life for good.

So, first things first, I slept with someone David was cool with, and then I called his parole officer and told him he did not live at my house. I also told the parole officer to change his address. The last step was moving out. I left that house to David's mother and brother and moved far away from him.

I felt somewhat lost when I left because I would no longer be seeing David, a major shift from seeing him almost every day. Even though I had gotten way too comfortable with everything, I had to do what was best for me. And with that, the chapter of David was finally closed for good.

Chapter 16

"Don't allow yourself to wake up with yesterday's issues troubling your mind. Refuse to live backwards and see every day as a new chapter" is a quote I love and read daily. I stumbled across this quote while running errands one day, and it has stuck with me ever since.

Even after everything I had been through, I knew I still needed to push forward and continue living my life to the best of my ability. I could not allow yesterday to stop me from living today.

After years of heartbreak after heartbreak, I had reached a point in my life where I was determined to do better. I was not smoking as much, I was barely drinking, and I had moved away from toxic behaviors and people.

I was on the road to recovery, recovering from anything and everything that had stopped me from succeeding. I was working a full-time job, and I was finally pursuing a career in modeling, one of my childhood dreams.

Everything was going well for me. I was happy, and for the first time in my life, I was not depending on a man to make me happy. I was simply enjoying being Keren.

During this time period, I had spoken to a photography studio about taking some headshots. I figured that was the first place I needed to start to break into modeling. But all of that changed one Friday evening in June 2003. I never made it to the studio.

I had borrowed my mother's car to pick up my check from my job, and to go to the photography studio. I was on my way to pick up my mother when the police stopped me at a safety check.

"I need you to pull over to the side," a short Hispanic man said as he waved cars through the line.

As I watched him, I wondered why he had waved me to the side. Soon after, I realized I was not wearing a seat belt.

Nearly in a full-blown panic, I did not know what I was going to do. I did not have a valid license, and I probably had a warrant because of a missed court date.

"Your license and registration, please," the officer requested when he walked back to the car.

"I don't have my license on me, sir," I told the officer.

"What's your name?" he asked.

"Brandi," I lied.

"What's your birthday?" he asked.

"9-8-84, I mean 9-12-84. I be getting my sister's birthday mixed up with mine sometimes."

The officer walked away from the car with a funny look on his face, like he knew I was lying.

I sat there in that car, nervous as hell, knowing I was about to go to jail.

The officer walked back up to the car with a small notepad in hand and asked, "What did you say your name was again?"

At that moment, I knew I was busted.

"Keren," I confessed.

"Why did you lie?" the officer asked.

"I thought I had a warrant," I admitted.

"Ma'am, you don't have a warrant, and if you wouldn't have lied, I would've just written you a ticket. But now I have to arrest you," he said to me.

I sat there thinking, *Fuck. My dumb ass just told that lie when all I had to do was tell the truth.*

"How did you know I was lying?" I asked the officer with disappointment in my eyes.

"Well, you looked very nervous, and you gave the wrong birthdate. I called your mom, and she gave me your name and said if anyone besides you have her car, they stole it," the officer explained.

What the hell? I'm going to jail because my mom told on me, I repeated in my mind. I would have laughed if I was not so furious at the moment.

Even though I was in jail only for twenty-four hours, I swear it felt like twenty-four months. I had never been in there long enough to put on a jumpsuit or to get locked into a pod. The jail was freezing cold and loud, and the food was utterly disgusting. I knew those twenty-four hours would be the last twenty-four hours I ever spent in a place that. I knew it was not a place for me, and I was going to do whatever it took to never return there.

In between working full time and taking care of my daughter, I had no time to do anything else, which was a good thing. There was no kicking it with my friends, and I was definitely not entertaining any guys. I was focused and headed down the right path. But you know when you are on the right path, the devil always tries to send distractions your way to make you veer off track. That is exactly what happened when I met John.

I met John when I went to my old block one day to visit a few friends. He lived in an apartment right below my cousin's apartment.

When I pulled up, John was sitting on the porch in some khaki cargo shorts and a blue and red striped polo shirt, with blue shoes to match. He was dark-skinned with a medium build and stood about 5'10" in height. Even though he was handsome and reminded me of Martin Lawrence, I was not checking for him.

His ass is too old anyway, I thought.

I sat on the porch with John and my cousin for about three hours that day. Within that time frame, I learned John was nine years older than me, worked as a barber, lived with his mom and uncle, had two kids but did not want anymore, and, of course, wanted to get to know me. Though I was not interested at first, the more we talked, the more I wanted to get to know him, too.

What started off as a free haircut, his way of trying to break the ice and get in good with me, quickly turned into a relationship, one I was not ready for but still embraced. I embraced him and his family.

In the beginning, it impressed me how close he was to his family. In the end, it was one of the things that hurt our relationship.

When I was twenty years old, exactly five months before my twenty-first birthday, I moved in with John, his mom, *and* his uncle.

On a sunny yet cool evening in October 2003, I was sitting on the porch with John's uncle, Lenny, smoking a blunt when John came outside and sat next to me.

"You know you're always over here, and we either spend nights here or at your house, so it would be better if you just move in over here," John said nonchalantly.

I took another puff of the blunt and passed it to John, and I just stared at the side of his head for a moment.

"So, you want me to move in with you over here?" I asked for clarification.

"Yeah, why not?" he asked, as if confused about why I was not jumping on the offer.

Yes, he made some valid points about me being over there all the time, and I really loved-liked him, so I did not mind it. But I also did not want to lose my independence, especially my own place, and move in not only with him but also with his momma and his uncle. This was something I definitely had to think about.

After one long week of weighing the pros and cons of moving in with John, I said to hell with it. I moved in with him and his family.

I was unsure if it was love, infatuation, or stupidity, but it had to be something to make me want to move into a two-bedroom apartment with three other people, three people who were not my family, three people whom I had just met.

Imagine waking up next to the man you share your world with, smelling his scent, looking into his sleepy eyes, and feeling the warmth of his body. Having that gives you a great sense of comfort, that is, until the newness wears off and you wake up to the smell of marijuana smoke and unwanted niggas invading your space.

"What's all that noise out there?" I asked John when I heard him walk back into our bedroom one morning.

"Oh, that's E and Dre," he replied as he grabbed some cigars from the dresser.

I glanced at the clock. "It's 9 a.m. Why are they over here already?" I asked him through my tired, cracking voice.

I was trying not to sound so annoyed, but I was pissed off big time. I had not even gotten up, washed my face, or brushed my teeth, yet there were already people over, trying to get high. As you can imagine, I was livid.

"Damn, did they sleep over here, and I didn't know about it?" I asked sarcastically.

"Here you go with your shit," John responded with an attitude.

I could not believe he was getting an attitude with me instead of with his friends for coming over so early in the morning, or that he would even want to be around the same people all day, every day.

Often, I wondered, *Damn, do they really even have women because how are they not upset they don't ever see their niggas*?

After stretching and shaking my head, I climbed out of bed, walked into the bathroom to complete my morning routine, and then marched to the kitchen to interrupt their little "He-Man Woman-Haters Club" meeting.

I walked into the kitchen, and all three of them were sitting there rolling up their blunts, wearing the same shit they had on the day before. Again, I shook my head, this time thinking they could accomplish so much more if they did not spend their days sitting around smoking all day.

"Is he your breakfast?" I asked, standing there in the middle of their sister circle with my hand on my hip, looking at them in disgust.

"Gone, Killa," John said.

Killa was the nickname John and his friends gave me because I would be on all their asses when they came over to the house. I would want them to leave, at least for a little while, just like I did then. There was never a day that went by that at least two of them were not at our house. The shit was frustrating me and pushing me away.

Trying my best not to go off, I sucked my teeth and asked for some money. Then I grabbed a blunt and headed out the door to leave John and his girlfriends alone.

While sitting on the porch enjoying the freshness of the air and the heat from the sun, I noticed kids playing outside and people sitting on their porches. Lenny, John's uncle, was already sitting outside on the porch with his coffee and his cigarette.

"Hey, Uncle Lenny," I greeted him.

"Good morning, Killa," he replied.

I rolled up my blunt, and then I lit it up, inhaled, and exhaled.

"You know, Uncle Lenny, I'm tired of living like this. This is not me, and I'm tired of all the company every day. I'm so ready to leave," I told him as I blew the weed smoke out of my mouth.

"I feel you, Killa. I don't know why he do some of the stuff he do," Uncle Lenny replied.

"I don't know, but the shit is getting old as hell, and he don't seem to give a damn, so I think it's time for me to make a change." I passed him the blunt, thankful to have at least one person I could talk to.

"Maybe you all should get a house of your own; maybe that would bring some of the company and traffic down. He not supposed to sell where he lay his head down anyway," Uncle Lenny said.

That's an interesting idea, I thought to myself.

"Yeah, imma have to talk to him about that; something is going to have to change."

Shortly after my conversation with Uncle Lenny, I sprang into action. I found a house and purchased a new car. Two months later, John and I moved into our own home. It was so nice, cozy, and peaceful. I did not have to worry about people all inside of the house. It was just me, John, and Charity, until I came home one day and realized one of John's nappy-headed-ass, so-called friends had kicked in our door.

I worked Monday through Friday, 8 a.m. to 5 p.m. One Tuesday evening, after John had picked me up from work, we drove straight home without making any extra stops. Once we arrived at the house, we noticed someone had kicked in our door.

"What the fuck? Stay here," John said to me when he noticed the door halfway opened.

I stood there pissed off, looking around, trying to see if I noticed anyone watching our house or anything out of the ordinary. While standing on the porch, I called out to John, "Is anyone in there?"

"No, the house is clear," he said.

After inspecting the house, we noticed the only things missing were a chain that was on the entertainment stand and a safe that was on the living room floor. Thankfully, the safe was empty because we had just gotten it.

"You know it had to be someone you deal with who came into the house," I told John.

"Yeah, it definitely had to be," he agreed with a scowl on his face.

For obvious reasons, we could not call the police, so we rigged the door closed. Then John got on the phone with some of his homies to come down to sit guard with him.

Having the door to our home kicked in reminded me of how it felt to have someone violate your space without your permission. Once images of my uncle crept into my mind, I suddenly felt cornered with nowhere to turn. There was no way I could continue living in that house. I did not feel comfortable or safe. I just wanted to leave.

Shortly after the break-in, frustration kicked back in because there we were, moving back to his momma's house, the last place I wanted to be.

"Can we talk?" I asked John one night after all his company had left the house.

"What's up?" he asked.

"I love you, but I'm sorry. I can't do this. I can't continue to live like this. I think we need a break, so I will be moving out and moving back home with my momma," I told him as politely as I knew how.

He stared at me for a moment, and then he relaxed his posture. "That's fucked up, but if that's what will make you happy," he replied, as if he was saying whatever.

"It's for the best," I told him.

He just nodded his head and turned his attention to the TV. That was my cue to start packing.

Within the next two days, I was no longer living in the house with John, and I was elated to be back at home with my mom.

♥

The longer I was away from John, the more I grew closer to another guy, someone I had a faint past with. It was not something I had planned on happening, but I was happy it was happening.

My blast from the past, Mr. ASAP, and I were on a whole different level; he was becoming my best friend. He had spent the night at my house once, not too long after I finally left Chucky Jr. alone. We did nothing except smoke together and fall asleep next to each other. I truly think he respected me, unlike so many other men I had met.

ASAP crossed my path again when I went to the gas station one morning to grab a Red Bull before heading to orientation for my new job. I spotted him walking into the store.

"Hey, beautiful," he said to me.

"Hello," I responded, instantly knowing who he was.

"What you doing out so early in the morning?" he asked.

"I had to stop and get me some caffeine before I headed to work," I told him.

"Yeah. Me, too," ASAP responded, smiling at me.

Does he even know who I am? I asked myself as I stared at him, a little puzzled.

"It's my first day today, and I have orientation."

"Wow, really? It's my first day today, too," he responded.

"Well, I hope you have a great day," I said to him as I paid for my Red Bull.

"You, too," he replied.

Seconds later, I walked out of the gas station and drove off.

Now ASAP had a smooth, milky brown complexion. He was a fine brotha with a fade haircut and waves, a gold tooth, and a medium build and height. His swag and demeanor put me in the mind of Jadakiss, and I loved Jadakiss!

After arriving at the workplace, I was sitting in the orientation classroom when about five minutes later, in walked ASAP. I looked at him and smiled, and he returned the gesture. He could not hide the confusion on his face, though.

Still smiling, he took a seat right next to me. "Wow, what's the odds of that?" he said.

"Yeah, that's crazy," I replied. *Maybe this is a sign*, I thought.

"Well, I guess we doing lunch together then, right?" he asked.

"Sure," I said, elated.

From that moment on, we were inseparable.

I eventually reminded ASAP of how we already knew each other. Even though he was shocked, he remembered everything once I told him.

The relationship, friendship, or whatever we had went on for months. I was happy with what we shared, and I did not want to lose it or for it to change, but it soon did.

On the morning of April 10, 2006, I walked outside of my mom's house, headed to work, when I noticed some red, long stem roses in my windshield wipers with a note attached. I picked up the roses and opened the note. It read: *I'm sorry for everything. I love you. Can we please talk? Love, John*. Though I smiled at the notion, I was a little taken aback by everything. I had so many questions flowing through my head that my time at work was just a blur.

After work, I drove over to John's house to see what he wanted to talk about. When I pulled up to the apartment, John was sitting on the porch with his mom and Uncle Lenny. John was still attractive to me, but I just did not know if I still loved him the same way.

I got out of the car, and before I could walk up to the porch, he trotted down the stairs.

"Can you take a ride with me?" John asked me.

"Where are we going?" I asked.

"Can you just take a ride with me? I want to talk to you for a second," he responded.

"Sure," I agreed, nervously. While I trusted John, my mind flashed back to Brian and Chucky Jr. I would be lying if I said I was not anxious.

Yet, we hopped into his truck and rode in silence for what seemed like forever.

"Where are you taking me, and why aren't you saying anything?" I asked him, finally breaking the silence.

"Just thinking," he responded.

I was looking out the passenger window when I noticed us pulling into the parking lot of the Ice Cream Shack, one of the best ice cream shops in Peoria.

"Come on," he said.

Still confused, I got out of the truck and followed him to the front counter. John ordered two ice cream cones, and then we sat at a table.

"You know why I chose this place to talk to you at?" he asked.

"No, I know this is where we had our first semi-date at, though," I responded.

"Exactly," he said. "I know we done had our ups and downs, and I know you 'bout sick of me, but I want you to know I love you, and I want to spend the rest of my life with you."

As he was pleading his case, he got down on one knee.

"Will you please do me the honor of being my wife?" he asked.

Instantly, I felt tears on my cheeks. I looked around and noticed there were people standing around watching us. Without even thinking twice, I turned back to him and said "yes".

He got up off his knee and took me into his arms and kissed me.

I said yes because I truly did love him, but deep down, I knew he was not ready. I knew nothing had changed, and I knew nothing would change by us saying "I do".

Even though I knew our lives would not change overnight, I wanted to give our relationship one more shot. But there was one problem: ASAP. I wondered how I was going to tell him, and if I was ready to leave him alone.

The moment I got some free time away from John, I called ASAP.

"Hey," I said as he answered the phone.

"What's up, love?" he replied.

I took a deep breath. "I hate to tell you this, and over the phone, but I need to tell you that John asked me to marry him, and I told him yes," I said, regretfully.

"You did what?" he asked me through what sounded like gritted teeth.

"I'm sorry." It was the only thing I could say.

"Wow," he responded.

"Do you forgive me?" I asked.

"Yeah, we good. Have a good life," he said before hanging up on me. Knowing that would probably be the last time I ever heard from him, I held the phone for a while.

I was so hurt because I knew I had hurt him. Of course, I had feelings for ASAP, and I knew we were happy, but I just had to be sure about John.

♥

A little over a month after John's proposal, I found out I was pregnant with my second and last child.

I was overjoyed when I found out I was pregnant, and I thought John would be, too, but he made some comments about wanting to know the specific date of conception, like I did not know who the hell my child's father was.

Those nine months were supposed to be some of the happiest times for us, but they were the most unpleasant times for me. Outside of the constant in and out of his company, living in the house with his momma again, and now his "supposed-to-be cousin" whom I could have sworn he was fucking, this nigga had the nerve to say he needed to get a blood test.

I knew I had made a mistake by taking John back and moving back in with him. Nothing had changed, except for me once being happy and now being miserable again. And there was only one way that could change: I would have to be the one to fix it.

John and I were together for a total of six years. Six long years. Yes, we had some good times, but the bad times seemed to outweigh the good ones. Though I was still present physically, I had checked out of our relationship both mentally and emotionally. I was over all the toxic madness, and I was over pretending like everything was okay.

I decided that once my baby was born, I was going to take a leap of faith, not only for a change of status, but also for a change of atmosphere. I was going to leave it all behind, all the pain, all the hurt, and all the drama.

On January 2, 2007, John woke up super early that morning to take his older daughter and son back home to their mother in Atlanta. They had been with us for Christmas break, and it was time for them to return to school.

John intended to drop them off and make a turnaround trip, but something about that morning just did not feel right.

"Can you wait one more day, please? What if I go into labor?" I asked him.

"You will be fine. I really need to get them down there so I can get on back home," he responded.

I said nothing else because I felt like it would be a losing battle with him, so I just lay there in the bed quietly.

"Goodbye, Keren," the kids said as they gave me a hug.

"I'll see you guys later. I love you," I said to them.

"Well, I'll see you when I get back," John said.

"Okay, drive safe and be careful," I told him.

After John and the kids left the house around 5 a.m., I went back to sleep. A sharp cramp in my stomach jolted me awake about three hours later.

"Uncle Lenny!" I yelled out.

John's uncle came rushing through the door. "What's wrong?" he asked me.

"I think I'm going into labor," I groaned. The pain that rushed through my body was the most excruciating pain ever. It felt like cramps on steroids.

"Oh, shit!" he said. "Let's go."

"I need you to call my mom," I urged Uncle Lenny. "Please let her know I need her."

Uncle Lenny went straight into panic mode, barely able to dial the number or find the car keys.

Thankfully, I made it to the hospital within five minutes. I was there for six hours before giving birth to my baby girl, Janice. And John was not there to witness any of it.

Even when John made it back to town, his first stop was not at the hospital to see his daughter. He went home to get some rest.

I know he was tired because he had just returned from a long turnaround trip, but he could have rested at the hospital. In my eyes, his first priority should have been coming to see his newborn child.

When I woke up the next morning, John was still not there, so I tried calling the house phone to see where he was. No answer.

I called his cellphone and the house phone over fifteen times. No answer from either phone.

Okay, I have a trick for that, I thought to myself.

"Hello," my friend Alley said when she answered the phone. Her boyfriend was cool with John.

"Hey, girl, I need you to do me a favor. Can you call John's house phone on three-way? Some reason they're not answering the phone," I explained.

"Of course," she said.

"Hello?" John's supposed-to-be cousin answered the phone seconds later.

I knew this bitch was screening the calls and saw it was me calling.

"Put John on the phone," I demanded.

"He sleep," she replied.

"I don't give a fuck! Wake his ass up and give him the phone," I screamed.

"Hello?" I heard John's voice next, and my blood boiled.

"Why the fuck has no one been answering the fucking phone all morning?" I yelled.

"I was tired. I'm just waking up," he said.

"Well, you need to get yo' ass up and get to this hospital and see your daughter."

"Okay, I'll be up there in a second."

I hung up the phone.

If ever I was on the fence about us and the decisions I was going to make, this incident made it perfectly clear what I needed to do.

How in the hell are you allowing someone to screen your girl's calls when she's in the hospital having your baby? I wondered.

In all honesty, that cousin should have gotten told off and put in her place, but I decided to keep my peace. And the fact that John did not say one peep about her let me know the truth.

With a newborn baby not even a day old yet, I realized John was not the man for me, and this thing between us was truly over. I realized it was time for me to move on with my life. That is exactly what I planned on doing as soon as I stepped foot outside of that damn hospital.

The relationship chapter with us is closed. I'm taking my kids, and I'm moving on without him.

I'm moving to Indiana.

I picked the phone back up and dialed quicker than I ever had before.

"Hello," my cousin Jimmy's voice boomed on the other end of the phone.

Holding my breath, I exhaled and then yelled into the receiver, "COME GET ME!"

To be continued . . .

♥

About the Author

First-time author Keonta Polk aspires to use her story as a source of inspiration for young girls facing adversity. Familiar with the struggles that accompany depression and low self-esteem, she aims to help young women know their worth, fill their hearts with love, and face the future with confidence. Believing that change begins with knowing and loving oneself, Keonta writes to give a voice to the voiceless, those who carry guilt and shame about the challenges they are often too afraid to express.

Born and raised in Peoria, IL, Keonta is a devoted mother of two and an assistant branch manager of a cash logistics company. She loves reading books, writing poetry, and enjoying the simple things in life.

Contact Info:

Facebook: Keonta Polk
Instagram & TikTok: @melaninkp
Email: keontapolk@outlook.com

Made in the USA
Columbia, SC
06 September 2024

41902383R00131